The Entomological Tales of Augustus T. Percival

PETRONELLA SAVES NEARLY EVERYONE

The Entomological Tales of *Augustus T. Percival*

PETRONELLA SAVES NEARLY EVERYONE

Dene Low

illustrations by Jen Corace

Houghton Mifflin
Houghton Mifflin Harcourt
Boston   New York   2009

Houghton Mifflin Books for Children is an imprint of Houghton Mifflin Harcourt
Publishing Company.

www.hmhbooks.com

The text of this book is set in Cochin.
The illustrations are pen and ink and ink wash on paper.

Library of Congress Cataloging-in-Publication Data is on file.
ISBN: 978-0-547-15250-9

Manufactured in the United States of America
QUM 10 9 8 7 6 5 4 3 2 1

To my wonderful husband and my children, grandchildren, and parents, who support me and are patient with me. To Mrs. Opal Owen, my sixth-grade teacher who started my writing career

Chapter One

In Which an Intruder Is Incoming

THERE IS SOMETHING TERRIBLY WRONG with Mr. Augustus T. Percival.

The wrongness can be traced to a particular occurrence at a specific time—12:47 and 32 seconds on May 26 in 1903, to be exact. (I had just looked at my watch.) The weather was unusually warm for the season, and so Mr. Percival— who is my uncle Augustus—a few select friends, and myself were gathered on the lawn in the south garden of my estate just outside London, enjoying a little nuncheon in honor of my sixteenth birthday.

At that precise time, Uncle Augustus laughed loudly at a rather mediocre joke—the one about the man with two heads who could eat only strawberry jam with one mouth and cheese curds with the other. At the very moment Uncle

Augustus opened his own mouth for a most unseemly guffaw (and Uncle Augustus is a very large man, so the rather moist open mouth made a massively large target), a beetle of enormous proportions flew into the orifice and was swallowed.

Unfortunately, we did not know what type or genus the beetle was, or a cure might have been effected. Uncle Augustus sat deathly still, with all signs of his former joviality banished. He set down his cup of tea undrunk, pushed away the plates piled high with crumpets and cucumber sandwiches, said "Perhaps I don't feel quite the thing after all," and departed to his room.

My other guests and I paused for an awkward moment, and then continued in polite conversation, just as those who occupy the upper echelons of society ought to do when faced with unusual circumstances. Then we, too, departed to our rooms for a nap to fortify ourselves for the evening's festivities.

NO ONE WAS more startled than I, when, several hours later, I saw Uncle Augustus on his hands and knees, groveling in the newly turned earth of the east garden. Rushing to see if I might be of some assistance to my beloved relation, I was

horrified to see him pounce, then hold up a wriggling centipede. Before I could do more than gasp, Uncle Augustus
dropped the squirming creature into his mouth—which I
have previously described all too graphically—and swallowed the cartilaginous body with seeming relish (the emo-
tion, not the condiment).

"Uncle Augustus . . ."

He beamed at me from his prostration in the dirt. "Ah,
my dear Eunice. So good to see you again."

I considered his greeting rather imbecilic, considering
that he was groveling in my garden and we'd only just parted
company a few hours before. Besides, he knew I preferred
to be called Petronella. Eunice is such an unfortunate name,
and I cannot imagine what came over my dear but deceased
parents when they gave it to me. Perhaps some sort of simul-
taneous apoplectic fit.

"Uncle Augustus," I said more severely, and pointed
toward the garden bed, which Thomas the gardener had
taken great pains to till in preparation for the dahlias I had
hoped to plant on Saturday. "What are you doing?"

Uncle Augustus frowned. He tapped one finger on his
chin, then waggled it at me thoughtfully. "I've been contemplating that myself. The question seems to be not so much
what I am doing, but what I've *become.* It appears I have developed an enormous appetite—"

"Yes, well, that is common knowledge," I could not help but agree.

"Ahem. Let me continue uninterrupted, if you please. It seems I have an enormous appetite for all things of the insect and arachnoid varieties." He caught a passing fly in one swift movement of his hand, popped it into his mouth, and chewed happily.

I could do naught but stare. For the first time in my life I was at a loss for words. The sight of Uncle Augustus's enormous jowls expanding and contracting with disturbing regularity was enough to make anyone stare, but that was not the cause of my distress. Over the years that he had been my guardian, I had become inured to the sight of Uncle Augustus eating. No, I was contemplating that it was my moral duty to render assistance to Uncle Augustus through this trial. Blood will out, as they say, and he was my blood relative, brother to my dear departed mother, whom I missed terribly. The question was, how was I to help him?

"Oh, Uncle," I said finally.

"Do not fret yourself, my child. I have examined myself rather thoroughly, and seem to be in fine fettle, except for this compulsion to eat crawling creatures." He eyed the ground next to him for a moment and grabbed a spider that had the misfortune to have ventured forth from its lair. It quickly shared the fate of the fly.

"You cannot possibly desire to continue in this state," I protested, concerned for his well-being.

"And why not? I feel better than I have in years." He used both hands to pluck a series of ants from the retaining wall about the garden plot, his fingers darting from the stones to his lips so rapidly I could scarcely see them except as a blur. I had never known Uncle Augustus to move so quickly. Indeed, there was a glow of health about him that I had not seen before.

"Could you please stop that . . . that . . . inhaling of those odious bugs and talk sensibly to me?"

Uncle Augustus paused and fixed his gaze on me most consideringly as one of his hands seemed to move of its own volition toward a pile of stones. He caught it with his other hand and held it tightly. Both hands shook with the effort of keeping still, and, for the first time, he seemed a trifle alarmed. "Why, no. I don't seem to be able to."

"Be able to what? Stop? Or talk sensibly?"

"Stop, of course. Nor do I see any reason why I should stop. And I feel that, under the circumstances, I am conversing quite rationally." He began sorting through the pile of stones. When he found a fat slug, he held it up triumphantly and then lowered it toward his gaping maw.

I could not watch him further, and so I turned my back, pressing my eyes shut in horror at the loud slurping noise that followed. "Uncle Augustus," I said through gritted teeth. "I cannot imagine that your behavior is at all socially acceptable. Surely that is a reason to want to stop gorging yourself on creeping crawling things."

"My dear Eunice —"

"Petronella!" I said.

"If you must . . . Petronella. Although your dear mother loved the name Eunice."

"Well, I do not — and neither did my father, which is why Petronella is my first name."

"Very well, then, Petronella. You have always been more concerned with the conventions of society than I have —"

"Unfortunately, that is so."

"Except when you interrupt. I must say this penchant you have for interrupting is most uncivil."

I was mortified to realize he was correct. "I apologize, dear uncle. My concern for you overwhelmed me to the point of rudeness."

He did not answer immediately, and when he did, he sounded as if he had just swallowed something. I shuddered to think what it was. "Apology accepted, dear child. However, I can see that my current state could be something of an embarrassment in polite company, which is especially problematic because my presence is required at this evening's event."

I swung around to face him, my mouth open in a perfect O of consternation. "Tonight! Oh, Uncle Augustus. This would have to happen today of all days, just when I am about to attend my coming-out party. James will be so disappointed." My hand flew to cover my mouth. "I mean, *Jane* will be so disappointed, and so will all the other guests."

Uncle Augustus seemed not to have heard my slip of the tongue—one that Dr. Freud would have made much of, if I understand his theories correctly—for my cherished relative seemed intent on going about his hunting. "And why should your little friends be disappointed?"

"We cannot possibly hold the party if you are in such a condition."

Pausing only long enough to fix me with a thoughtful gaze, Uncle Augustus said, "Fear not, dear Eunice, er . . . Petronella. We shall not deprive your friends of your company. I have thought of a plan."

Chapter Two

In Which There Are
Coming-Out Complications

"AVOID THE STRAWBERRY TRIFLE. IT is exactly the same shade as the Countess of Wilberforce's tresses, and I cannot recommend it," said James in my ear as he passed close to my shoulder.

I could just hear him over the buzz of hundreds of partygoers in the tent Uncle Augustus had hired to grace the grounds of my estate for my coming-out party. The guests looked resplendent under the lamps hanging from the tent poles, around which flitted numerous moths. I hoped Uncle Augustus would not disgrace himself, and me in the process, with those flying insects. His plan was to bandage his hands to keep himself from seizing bugs, but I was not confident of the efficacy of this method. Unfortunately, my fears proved well grounded. For at that moment, I saw my uncle's head bob above the crowd three times in succession near the far-thest tent pole. All the moths near that light were then gone. I turned quickly to James, hoping he had not noticed.

I said to James, "Lord Sinclair, old thing. How perfectly rude of you to remark on the countess's tresses and yet say nothing of how well you like mine." I arched my neck to show off my curls piled artfully on top of my head, as befit-ted a young lady who no longer was considered a schoolgirl. I simpered at him most seriously, although I did have to cut off a laugh as I caught sight of the Countess of Wilberforce holding a plate of strawberry trifle that was indeed the same shade as her hair. Wicked James.

James's eyes twinkled, and his mouth curved in a smile that had smitten me since I was five and he was nine. If only he were not Jane's brother—brother of my bosom friend—he might consider me as more than a younger sister. But fate plays cruel games with hearts and shows no remorse. If I were to have him notice me at all, it should have to be as a sister, and I should have to be content with that or nothing, and to have nothing of James would be the cruelest fate of all.

I suddenly remembered Uncle Augustus. I looked about and thought I saw the top of his head bouncing above the crowd. In fact, I was sure of it when I saw that where several moths had been flitting about a lamp in the general direction of the lights near the orchestra, now there were none. Oh, rubbish. Uncle Augustus had promised that his plan was foolproof. If anyone noticed, I would be ruined.

James hooked his arm through mine and propelled me toward the refreshment table. "Allow me to escort you, Miss Arbuthnot. I do believe my sister, Jane, is hovering disconsolately by the punch, awaiting the chance to speak with you," he said so all around us could hear. Then, in my ear, James whispered, "And you have said nothing about my hirsute splendor. Your curls, by the way, are ravishing, and if I were not currently enamored of a chit playing the part of Isabelle in the West End, I would be in danger of losing my heart. Sixteen suits you."

Of course he did not mean it for a minute, although my heart did give a sort of flip-flop at his suggestion. I calmed myself resolutely. Everyone knew James held his string of actresses before him like a shield protecting him from matrimony, much to the dismay of many a *mama* who would like to mark him as the property of one of her daughters. His fortune, title, and career in the Home Office made him a most eligible bachelor.

I peered at James from the corner of my eyes and studied his dark waves arranged carelessly and held in place with brilliantine, of which I could just catch a whiff. "I would tell you how perfectly splendid you are tonight if I did not think you already had an overly high opinion of yourself," I replied.

He clutched his starched white shirt front as a laugh escaped him. "Touché. I perceive the danger of trying to preen in front of such an old friend." He emphasized the word "old," and I knew he remarked on my age. I sighed inwardly. I may have reached adulthood, but I truly never would be seen as anything more than a younger sister by James.

As we were quite near the refreshment table, I disengaged myself from his arm and sailed toward Jane. "Miss Sinclair, darling. What an absolutely gorgeous gown. That shade of rose does set off your complexion to perfection."

Jane turned from the conversation she was having with Georgie Grimsley, a most inconsequential young man. It was well known that he was looking for a wealthy wife to pay his family's debts. Mischief lurked in Jane's eyes, and I knew she had been thoroughly enjoying making sport of him. "Why, Miss Arbuthnot. Congratulations on your birthday. And as for your gown, it is quite magnificent, is it not, James? It complements the blue of her eyes most becomingly." She cocked her head and smiled at me while she held her bottom lip with her even white teeth.

It was all I could do not to laugh. We had practiced that

look in the mirror just that afternoon before I had found Uncle Augustus in the garden. We had also examined each other's frocks and rehearsed what we would say.

"I say, Miss Arbuthnot. You do look splendid," young Grimsley interrupted without letting James reply to his sister, which I thought shockingly rude.

"And how do you do, Mr. Grimsley?" I asked a touch coldly.

He was saved the trouble of answering because of the commotion by the tent entrance as a woman of magnificent proportions and jewelry entered. She was on the arm of a mustachioed gentleman with two bejeweled medals hanging on velvet ribbons around his neck.

"Ah, I expected that Dame Carruthers would be here to-night along with Generalissimo Reyes-Cardoza of Panama," murmured James. "I must go and pay my respects. It is the responsibility of the Home Office to ensure his safety. Excuse me, ladies."

Jane and I watched James make his way through the throng of guests who were staring at Dame Carruthers, quite the most famous person at my party and the most resplendent. She was also the most unexpected. I wondered who had invited her and the generalissimo. What with Panama on the verge of rebellion against Colombia, I should have thought the newly made dame would have shied away from any contact with rebels against a sovereign nation. Perhaps his medals had attracted her.

Of course, James would have to greet her. He knew all the theatrical people, especially the famous ones, and Dame Carruthers fit that category like a kid glove, much as her gown fit her. She had been given the title by King Edward himself, a man also known to have a penchant for actresses. I supposed I should have to greet her, too, since it was my party. Now that I was thoroughly grown up, I would have to play hostess for my own soirees and those of Uncle Augustus.

At the thought of my esteemed uncle, I was reminded of his aberrant behavior. Wherever could that man be? As far as I could see, nearly all the moths in the tent were gone. I would have to find him once I greeted my unexpected guests.

I followed James toward the dame and her escort, dragging Jane along and quite ignoring trivial Grimsley, whom I could hear sputtering by the punch bowl.

My guests parted as if I were Moses and they were the Red Sea. A few offered birthday greetings. I nodded pleasantly and smiled in reply as I proceeded, feeling as if I were a princess in a procession in one of the Baltic countries. Not that I'd ever been to a Baltic country, but one can imagine.

"And here is the birthday girl herself. How charming you look, my dear. Ah, to be in the first bloom of youth again," Dame Carruthers gushed as she pinched my cheek.

I felt all of three years old, which is probably exactly what she intended, the wicked old witch. James had to turn away to restrain a sudden fit of coughing. If he'd been any closer, I would have kicked him, surreptitiously of course, but with sufficient force to lame him for a week.

Instead, I smiled ingenuously and replied, "Why, thank you, Dame Carruthers. You are most kind. Your opinion matters a great deal to me. One cannot help but admire someone who has held audiences enthralled for *so many years*. And may I add that you look absolutely splendid tonight and put the rest of us to miserable shame."

James required pounding on the back by Generalissimo Reyes-Cardoza.

At the mention of her age, Dame Carruthers's face darkened, but she proved herself a competent actress and smiled at Jane, taking her by the hand, and saying over her shoulder to James, who had nearly caught his breath, "Dear Lord Sinclair, this must be your little sister. She is like a dainty Dresden china image of you when you were younger. Do introduce us."

I have to admit that Dame Carruthers described Jane perfectly. She is quite the most beautiful girl I know.

James straightened his shirt front and did his duty in acknowledging the beauty of his sister. Jane said all that was proper, although I could tell she felt like scratching the actress's eyes out. I knew we would have a jolly time recounting our adventures in our rooms after the party.

"And may I also present Generalissimo Alejandro Reyes-Cardoza," said Dame Carruthers. "The generalissimo is escorting me so that he may meet all the right people. Generalissimo, Miss Arbuthnot."

"I'm pleased to meet you," I said while the generalissimo bent over my gloved hand and clicked his heels.

"The pleasure is all mine, señorita." He smiled at me so appreciatively, I felt myself blush. I was struck by the thought that if he should ever shave off his ridiculous mustache, he would nearly rival James in the category of masculine splendor.

Then Dame Carruthers surprised me no end when she asked, "Dear Miss Arbuthnot, may I ask where that most attractive uncle of yours is hiding himself?"

It was my turn to cough and need pounding on the back, which James did with more force than gallantry. I glanced about, wondering how many uncles she thought I had. There was only Uncle Augustus here, and I could scarcely call him attractive. As much as I adored him, I was always astonished at the reactions women in all stations of society had to Uncle

Augustus. Although he reminded me of a bullfrog, those of the fairer sex simply flocked to him. I caught sight of my uncle by the orchestra platform and was astonished further. I could clearly see that he had stuffed both bandaged hands under his armpits and was shaking badly.

Suddenly he lunged toward the moths near the lamp hanging on the center tent pole, compelled beyond his capacity to resist. The pole toppled, and the tent billowed down on my screaming guests.

Chapter Three

In Which Dame Carruthers Is Doomed

TO HAVE ONE'S TENT FALL on one's guests at one's coming-out party could be considered a crowning cataclysm. One would be expected to be unable to hold one's head up in polite society after such a debacle. As it was, I could not hold my head up because a great deal of tent canvas was weighing it down.

Muffled screams, curses, and calls for help filled the night air. At least I supposed they did. The air was filled with *something*, for I was not getting enough of it myself. If I did not act soon, I would suffocate. In a most inelegant fashion I wriggled between writhing bodies and folds of fabric. Eventually, after enduring some of the most unacceptable language directed at me each time I elbowed someone accidentally, I thrust my no-longer-coiffured head out from under the collapsed tent and gasped for breath. I dragged myself out and stood gaping at the heaving sea of canvas before me.

One of the underchefs, carrying a large platter of cold roast beef, hurried toward me from the direction of the house. "Mademoiselle, what has happened?"

I grabbed the carving knife from the platter and slit the canvas in several places just as Armond, my chef, would slice the crust of a particularly tasty pastry pie. People popped up everywhere I cut, including a not-so-resplendent James.

"I say, old stick," he said when he saw the knife in my hand, "most resourceful. Thanks awfully." He clambered up and away from the still-heaving tent, took the knife from me, and set to work freeing the rest of the guests.

Once freed and in full view of each other, my guests' behavior ran the gamut from stoicism to histrionics. The Countess of Wilberforce fainted twice. (The second time was undoubtedly because not enough people noticed her the first time.) She would not have wanted them to watch her had she seen the strawberry trifle slathered down her gown and dotting her hair, although the trifle was almost invisible among her curls. The stoic ones, led by James, helped other victims escape from the debris.

One of the last to emerge was Uncle Augustus, looking dazed. Bandages trailed from his hands, leaving his fingers unfettered. A moth fluttered by, which he absently plucked from the air and deposited in his mouth. He chewed thoughtfully as he surveyed my catastrophic coming-out party.

"Oh, Uncle Augustus," I said, shaking my head. I felt as if I might weep at any moment. My perfect night was ruined.

Uncle Augustus turned toward me with the expression of a small boy caught with a sack full of wet cats ready to be deposited in his governess's bed. At least I imagine that is what a small boy with a sack full of cats would look like—my education is woefully lacking in some areas.

"So sorry." He gulped.

I shuddered.

Jane walked up to me and slipped her arm through mine. How she managed to look exactly the same as she had before the calamity, I shall never know. But then, Jane always appears to have stepped out of a band box. I was surprised to see her laughing.

"This is the most splendid party I have attended in simply ages. It will be all the thing to talk about for six months at least. Everyone will have to claim to have been here if only to top everyone else's stories of how they barely managed to escape with their lives. We must keep an account of the stories and notice how they grow with each telling. It will keep us vastly amused."

I managed to smile a little. "Even so, one does not like to be the provider of such stories, no matter how entertaining." But I did feel better. Jane has that effect.

Uncle Augustus appeared to recover his spirits as well. He flitted into the shrubbery after another moth, seemingly without a care in the world except the pursuit of dinner. As it happened, I was beginning to feel the first pangs of hunger myself, having been deprived of the strawberry trifle and punch.

"I cannot find Dame Carruthers or Generalissimo Reyes-Cardoza. We must find them soon. My superiors in the Home Office will have my head if anything happens to him," James announced quietly as he came toward us.

At that moment I noticed a piece of paper nailed to a nearby tree and illuminated by the fairy lights strung about the garden. James and Jane both looked in the direction of my gaze.

"By George. I wonder . . ." said James, and we all approached the tree as if hypnotized.

Rather shaky handwriting wobbled across the paper, spelling out an ominous message:

Dame Carruthers and Generalissimo Reyes-Cardoza are in our power. You will follow the

directions that will come to you exactly or they will be doomed.

At the bottom of the page was a purple and turquoise splotch with wings and feelers.

"What is such an unusual butterfly doing affixed to the paper?" I asked James and Jane, pointing to the splotch.

At that instant, Uncle Augustus leaped between us and the tree. His right hand, trailing bits of bandage, snatched the butterfly from the message. He swallowed it in one gulp. Then, without so much as an apology, he leaped back into the shrubbery and vanished.

Chapter Four

In Which There Is an Inspector in the Garden

ALTHOUGH ONE MAY HAVE STACKS of money, not to mention an impeccable social position, there are times when one wishes for the homely pleasure of encircling parental arms. Such was the case when I surveyed the scene of the crime in the brightening dawn while being interrogated by Scotland Yard. I only hoped Inspector Higginbotham and his lackey Sergeant Crumple did not notice, as I did, the occasional rustle of bushes or the swaying of tree branches, which could only mean that Uncle Augustus was breakfasting.

"My dear Miss Arbuthnot, it would help immeasurably if we could speak to your uncle. Not only is he your guardian, but we've been told that he is also the means by which the tent collapsed. Pray tell us where we might find him," said Inspector Higginbotham, his jowls swinging below his chins with each syllable. If Uncle were a bullfrog, the inspector would surely be a bloodhound. Fittingly so, I might add.

I had visions of Uncle Augustus popping up from the petunias to capture a tasty morsel and became instantly certain that Inspector Higginbotham should not talk to my unfortunate relative. How could I explain such a circumstance? What would society have to say? Besides, I would not care to see Uncle Augustus hauled off to prison, or worse, to Bedlam, simply because he had a penchant for insects. 'Twould be most unfair and uncomfortable as well, for both Uncle and myself. I was having enough trouble trying to think of how to explain Uncle Augustus's condition to James and Jane, as I should have to once the detectives from Scotland Yard had gone. The two of them were already drawn to stare at said bushes and trees in bewilderment instead of paying attention to the interrogation, and besides, they had seen Uncle devour the insect on the note.

However, I could not betray him to the Yard. Several alternatives to producing Uncle to the detectives presented themselves to my mind. I could faint, but I was quite sure that James would take sadistic pleasure in waving a burned feather under my nose if I did, and burned feathers are immensely unpleasant. No, fainting would not do. I could make up some story about Uncle having gone missing at the same time as Dame Carruthers and Generalissimo Reyes-Cardoza, but Uncle was not mentioned in the note, and James and Jane might let it slip that they had seen him since. The other ideas were equally worthless. Instead, I decided to tell the truth . . . of a sort.

"I'm sure my uncle Augustus will be with us shortly. He is currently searching the grounds," I said. Indeed, the hawthorn bushes at the entrance to the maze moved suspiciously, and I caught a glimpse of a formally attired leg disappearing behind them. I moved slightly to one side so that the inspector would have his back to the hawthorns in order to look at me.

"He's more'n likely in cahoots wiv them kidnappers, thet's wot I fink," said Sergeant Crumple.

The inspector stiffened and bent a look of disapproval on his junior officer. "You will keep such thoughts to yourself, Crumple."

"I think the intrepid Sergeant Crumple has come up with a most intriguing idea. Please do not reprimand the man for doing his duty, dear Inspector Higginbotham," Jane simpered as she fluttered her eyelashes at the superior officer and then at the junior. "Don't you think so, James?"

Both James and I stared in surprise at Jane's sally into the fray.

James seemed at a loss. His majestic brow furrowed in

that endearing way he has when he is puzzled. Even in my extremity, I could not help but notice his charms.

Inspector Higginbotham harrumphed a few times and muttered something about "dear Miss Sinclair" under his breath, but he was clearly pleased by Jane's attentions. Sergeant Crumple turned crimson and could only stare at his much worn shoes, which appeared to have been tied with packing twine.

"My darling sister, surely you jest," James said.

"Not in the slightest, dear brother." Jane continued, "You do mean, of course, that Miss Arbuthnot and her uncle staged the coming-out party entirely for the purpose of kidnapping Dame Carruthers and Generalissimo Reyes-Cardoza, did you not, Sergeant Crumple?"

James was more bewildered than ever. "But Dame Carruthers and Generalissimo Reyes-Cardoza were not even on the guest list. How could it have been planned?"

"Yes, not only were they not on the guest list, I wonder how they heard about my party," I said as I nervously paced back to where Jane was standing so that Inspector Higginbotham must turn to attend to us. Uncle was now on his hands and knees following some repulsive creature along the garden path near the fountain, not far from the collapsed tent directly behind the inspector. Fortunately, Crumple was busy staring at Jane with a look of dismay. It was obvious, even to him, that Jane's explanation and therefore his accusation were absolutely ridiculous.

"Exactly," said Jane.

"Ahem."

We all focused on James, who had gone nearly as red as Sergeant Crumple.

"I'm afraid I must confess that I invited them," said James, ruining his hirsute splendor as he clasped his hair in both hands. "My superiors at the Home Office put me in charge of entertaining the generalissimo and ensuring his safety, and I thought he would be safe at Miss Arbuthnot's party. I will be in terrible trouble at the news that he and Dame Carruthers have disappeared."

Sergeant Crumple grabbed James by the arm. "Oi've got 'im, Inspector. No need to look furver. 'E probly 'as gambling debts and needs the ransom money. Wot have ye done wiv 'em?" He gave James's arm a shake.

"Here, here. Give off, man," said James as he disengaged himself from the overzealous officer. "Because I invited Dame Carruthers and Generalissimo Reyes-Cardoza to the party does not mean I am the one responsible for their kidnapping. Rather, it means that one of them must have mentioned their attendance at the event to the perpetrators, thereby presenting the perfect opportunity for them to be snatched away. Besides, I have no gambling debts. That would be most reprehensible."

But the good sergeant was not to be done out of a suspect so easily. "And wot, may I ast, would be the motiff for them to be snatched, as you say?"

"Yes, just what would be the motive for kidnapping, if it were not for ransom?" asked Inspector Higginbotham.

With an air of disdain, James dusted off the sleeve that had been crumpled by Crumple. "Actually, if you had been following the rumblings of current affairs, you would know of the problems over the Suez Canal that could halt British trade by sea with our colonies in the East."

I furrowed my brow in incomprehension. "What does the Suez Canal have to do with Panama's rebellion against Colombia? And what does dear England have to do with either?" The inspector, sergeant, and Jane looked equally befuddled.

James answered, "Because of trouble with the Suez Canal, we have need of the construction of the Panama Canal by the Americans to ensure British dominance of the high seas, and that won't happen unless the Panamanians win their independence from Colombia. There, I fear, is your motive. We are dealing with a tangled web of international intrigue."

27

Chapter Five

In Which the Aberration Is Explained

IT IS AN ESPECIALLY PAINFUL experience to explain to one's dearest friends that one's uncle has become an aberration. Jane did not easily come to terms with Uncle Augustus's propensity for devouring disgusting creatures, but James was immensely helpful. Once the Yard detectives left, he offered to help me capture Uncle Augustus, who had been flitting happily in the shrubberies all night and morning gorging himself on who knew what.

James dashed to his home and soon returned with an old straitjacket he said came from his Eton days. "Straitjackets were all the rage at the time," he told me, although I could not imagine what use they would have been for schoolboys. But perhaps it was better that I could not imagine it, considering what I do know of boys, James in particular.

"Whatever the case, I am grateful you have it now. I last heard Uncle Augustus crashing about in the arboretum. Let us hope he is still there so we might apprehend him," I said, following a trail of broken twigs among the privet hedges, evidence of Uncle's nocturnal depredations. I carried a pillow slip, which I hoped to sling over my unfortunate relative's head while James garbed him in the straitjacket.

"I must say you've held up rather well, old potato." James smiled at me. My traitorous heart flip-flopped, and I wondered if I should ever be free of my obsession with him.

A clatter, as if small pebbles were being dislodged, sounded on the other side of a hydrangea, followed by a most vulgar belch.

"Shh." I held my finger to my lips. James and I nodded to each other, and we went our separate ways. I crept around one side of the hydrangea while James skulked around the other.

Uncle Augustus was in the act of jovially breakfasting on an anthill, a look of complete contentment on his countenance. "Aaargh!" he shouted as I threw the pillow slip over his head. A shower of ants flew from his fingers and scurried away. I hoped they were cognizant of the fragility of their fate and suitably grateful at being freed.

James leaped forward, deftly slipped the straitjacket onto Uncle's arms, and had him trussed up in a moment.

My opinion of James was further improved when he picked up Uncle Augustus as if he were light as a feather and carted him off to the morning room, where Jane was partaking of some dry toast and weak tea to steady her nerves.

James deposited Uncle on the sofa and sat on him, ignoring his protests. In reality, Uncle Augustus was no lightweight, so for James to heft him about so easily made me wish I had gone to Brighton last summer with the Sinclairs when they had invited me. Then I could have watched James cavorting in the sea using those estimable muscles. If they invited me again this summer, I would be sure to go.

"I do thank you both for aiding us in our time of need," I said to James and Jane. I mournfully observed my dear relative as he struggled with his bonds. "I don't quite know what to do, what with the dame and generalissimo kidnapped and Uncle in such a state. I have no faith in the Yard solving this mystery. The detectives who came to investigate seemed like veritable simpletons. And poor Uncle . . ." I waved my hand feebly in his direction. There really was no need to explain further.

Jane put down her teacup with a tiny clink that bespoke a certain resoluteness. "I have been thinking of a solution. It is quite possible that we can gain assistance with both problems at the same source. James, did you not have a professor of entomology who was something of a world-famous authority?"

"Brilliant idea," said James. "For a sister, you are not half shabby. Professor Lepworthy would be just the ticket."

"PREPOSTEROUS!" SHOUTED PROFESSOR Lepworthy, his toupee sliding to one side of his monstrously shiny bald head. He swung around in his desk chair to retrieve a book from the case behind him, and the toupee slid back, coming to rest only slightly askew.

"Of course Uncle Augustus's condition is preposterous," I said rather acerbically, and James and Jane agreed with me.

"Not your uncle Augustus. He is not what is preposterous," retorted Professor Lepworthy, rapidly thumbing through the volume he had just retrieved and tossing it aside. His toupee dipped over his left eye as he twirled in his chair and reached for another book. When he swung back toward his desk, the hairpiece settled in place once more. I wondered if he'd had the hairy mop specially trained.

"Not Uncle Augustus?" Jane and James and I chimed together.

Professor Lepworthy stopped thumbing and shouted, "Aha!" Then he stuck his nose quite close to the book and stared intently. "No, indeed. Your uncle's condition is quite common in the outer marshes of Tou-eh-mah-mah Island, off the coast of Panama. The antidote is simple, actually. He must steep one of those beetles in a mixture of crocodile dung and the juice of the anaphtile plant and then drink the whole concoction while rotating on his rump and singing "Kwop-a-phah-mee" in twelve-tone the entire time. The only real difficulty is in finding a suitable anaphtile plant. It has to be one with flowers shaped like the Egyptian god Anubis, or the antidote will not work. It is my contention that the presence of a flower in the shape of Anubis is definitive proof that the Egyptians settled parts of the Americas."

I stared at James and Jane and they stared back. My high opinion of the idea of going to see the professor was starting to sink, even if he was reputed to know every insect on our planet like members of his own family. To my eye the professor was as batty as my uncle.

James must have noticed my incredulous expression, for he whispered, "Patience. You are witnessing a genius at work."

The aforementioned Uncle Augustus struggled under James, who was sitting on him on the professor's settee. "I will not drink any such concoction." Uncle Augustus seethed. "I feel perfectly fine."

Then his voice turned into peevish whining. "Speaking of perfectly fine, there are several rather fine specimens of insect over there on that wall. You wouldn't consider moving me a tad closer, would you, and unwrapping just one hand?"

For the first time I realized that Uncle Augustus might see the cases full of carefully labeled insects on pins as several courses of supper. I joined James on the settee and took hold of one of Uncle's legs so he could not get a good purchase on the floor, heave James from his straitjacketed body, and wriggle into proximity of one of those cases. Jane took hold of the other leg. We should have thought of a way of binding his enormous mouth, which could do as much damage as his hands.

I patted Uncle's head. "There, there, Uncle. The anthill will still be there when we get home, and Moriarty saw some termites in one of the cottages in the village. The tenants will be ever so grateful to you if you could rid their homes of the pests."

Uncle Augustus brightened and stopped struggling. "Do you think so? I hadn't thought of termites. There might be thousands of them. Millions, even. And if they are in one cottage, they might be in others. I was beginning to fear that

I would run out of delicacies on your estate in short order and I should be forced to search farther afield. But termites . . ." He hummed happily to himself, going off into what I could only think of as a termite-infested trance.

James bit off a chuckle, but Jane looked away politely. She always did have more delicate sensibilities than her brother.

"Yes, yes! Here it is! But it is preposterous." Professor Lepworthy shook the book before us, pages flapping within an eighth of an inch of his toupee, which had jerked up to the top of his head, leaving a great deal of gleaming skin between it and his eyebrows. "Look here. There can be no mistake."

We rushed to his desk and looked, forgetting Uncle Augustus. That is, we forgot him until we heard a peculiar thumping coming from the direction of the nearest glass case. Uncle Augustus was throwing himself at the case, evidently in an attempt to break the glass.

James sighed and picked Uncle Augustus up from the floor. He deposited my uncle in a chair, to which he tied him with the ends of the straps from the straitjacket. *I really must go to Brighton with the Sinclairs. Such muscles.* But duty intruded on my ruminations. Accordingly, I turned my attention back to the professor's book.

There, on the page in front of us, was an exact replica of the insect we had seen slightly squashed on the ransom note before Uncle Augustus ate it—the insect, not the paper. The insect was a butterfly of some sort, with wings that had a purple background and bright yellow and turquoise markings that spelled "Phui!"

Jane cleared her throat. "Ahem. It really is quite preposterous. Imagine having a word spelled out on a butterfly."

Professor Lepworthy looked at Jane as if she were an imbecile. "That is not what is preposterous. There is an entire genus of butterflies with words spelled out on their wings. Why, the Tanzanian novella butterfly has entire chapters written in Hindi. Of course, you have to read them with a magnifying glass, but they are well worth the trouble—very action packed. Sometimes the stories continue for generations. I have heard of entomologists, though, who have gone crazy because the last novella generation in an area died out before the end of the story—"

I interrupted. "Most fascinating, Professor Lepworthy, but we are more interested in why this particular butterfly you pointed out to us is preposterous." Uncle had said I was good at interrupting, and I felt as if I should put the skill to good use.

"Of course. To the point, and all that. If you must know

35

what is preposterous, it is not the butterfly itself, but where it comes from." He paused as if for dramatic effect, which was spoiled by his toupee slipping back farther.

"Which is . . . ," James, Jane, and I all said in concert.

"Tou-eh-mah-mah Island. The same place your uncle's beetle came from. I say, having two insects come here from an island thousands of miles away is . . . is . . ."

"Preposterous," we said.

Chapter Six

In Which a Truce Is Negotiated

WHEN ONE'S CHERISHED GUARDIAN HAS become a social pariah with no aspirations to change, one must reconsider one's personal goals. With circumstances as they were, my future had the brilliance of squashed toadstools. I was forced to envision my treasured dream of a London season receding over the horizon as if on the wings of an elusive Tou-eh-mah-mah butterfly unless Uncle Augustus's dietary preferences returned to normal, posthaste.

My problem was that I had no suitable female relations whom I could trust to sponsor me, with the operative word being *suitable.* There were two aunts on the Arbuthnot side, but the only way I would ask them for help was if Great Britain were to sink into the sea, as did Atlantis of old, and I were stranded in a leaky lifeboat—and even then I might choose to swim. Jane and James's mother would no doubt take me on, but she was in India visiting one of her old school chums. No, it would be easiest if I had a hale and hearty Uncle Augustus.

"I feel fit as a fiddle, I tell you," said Uncle Augustus as he leaped lightly from the seat of a Jacobean chair to the top of a Louis XIV armoire, both of which had graced the yellow sitting room in my home for generations. My ancestors were most likely turning in their graves at Uncle's treatment of heirlooms, and if they weren't, I was.

"So I see," I said. I took a bite of one of Armond's delectable muffins. It had a calming effect.

Uncle scrabbled about atop the armoire. "Did you know that the housekeeping staff doesn't clean up here? There were several dead spiders and flies and at least ten moths."

"Were?" I asked and then thought better about pursuing the subject. Resolutely brushing muffin crumbs from my fingers, I said, "Uncle, do you think we might have a little chat?"

Uncle Augustus caught the chandelier and swung nimbly into the chair across the tea table from me. "A tête-à-tête, as it were?"

"Yes. Now that everyone has gone and we are alone, I thought we could discuss your condition."

His brow furrowed. "Are you still trying to persuade me to drink that witch doctor's potion of crocodile dung and other bally ingredients?"

"Well —"

"I won't do it. I've never felt better in my life."

"Yes, but —"

"Look here. My old cricket injury has vanished. No more rheumatism in the knees or anywhere else, for that matter. It's as if I were twenty years younger." Uncle hopped about the room, first on one foot and then the other, to demonstrate.

I sighed. "That's wonderful, but —"

"It's more than wonderful. It's jolly magnificent!" Uncle snatched a fly from the air and transferred it into his mouth. Indeed, he looked as though he had been rejuvenated. I, on the other hand, felt one hundred years old. It was as if our roles were reversed.

"Uncle, you do realize that now you are interrupting me?"

He didn't look the least bit repentant. "What is it you wanted to say?"

"I merely wanted to discuss —"

A rapping on the French doors caught my attention. Through the window panes I spied the gleaming pate of Professor Lepworthy.

I let the professor in. "Why, Professor. Whatever are you doing out there? Did no one answer the front door?"

Professor Lepworthy entered without bothering to answer. All his attention seemed to be focused on my uncle. "I have been thinking," he announced as if that was all we needed to know.

Uncle Augustus strode forward and grasped Lepworthy's hand. "Welcome, sir."

"Augustus, may I call you Augustus?"

"Certainly," said Uncle.

"Please call me Maximus."

"Maximus, then. Come in and sit down." Uncle Augustus pulled a chair out and the professor sat.

Professor Lepworthy laid an enormous book on the tea table. The title was *Insectile Creatures*. "I have something here that may be of great use to you in two ways, Augustus." Next to the book he placed a box of waxed paper.

"What's this?" I asked. I did not see how those two objects could possibly help our present situation.

Uncle leafed through the book, pausing to look at some of the pictures. "Yes, Maximus. It does whet the old appetite. But what good is that?"

"Hunter-gatherers," Professor Lepworthy stated as if the term explained everything.

"Hunter-gatherers?" I repeated with raised eyebrows.

"Say what?" said Uncle Augustus.

"The Tou-eh-mah-mah people are hunter-gatherers. When they are in the same state as you, Augustus, they gather insects in finely woven picnic baskets to take with them wherever they go, thus avoiding the frantic compulsions you exhibit," the professor explained.

"He can scarcely carry a basket everywhere in polite society. It would be remarked on," I said.

"Ah, but if he had a book about his new interest in insects, people would merely consider him a trifle eccentric," said the professor.

Uncle Augustus picked up the waxed paper and waved it about. "And if that book had several insects pressed between bits of waxed paper, it would be a veritable Tou-eh-mah-mah picnic basket."

"You catch on quickly, Augustus." The two men smiled at each other. They were quite obviously kindred spirits.

"But that does nothing to alter the situation. True, Uncle Augustus could go about more easily, but he would still be in the same state," I protested.

"And a happy state that is," Uncle mumbled.

I appealed to the professor. "Can't you do something?"

"I brought the book." The professor tapped *Insectile Creatures*.

"Which does nothing but enable him to continue as he is,"

41

I said. I could see my London season receding farther and farther into the distance.

Lepworthy nodded. "True," he said. "It seems but a temporary solution. Augustus cannot carry such a large tome about forever, but it should do for now."

"Carrying it shouldn't be too hard," said Uncle. He hefted the book under one arm and jumped from the tea table to the Jacobean chair and back without any difficulty. "Ha!" he said triumphantly. "And double ha."

I considered what the professor had said. As a solution, the book was inconvenient. Perhaps Uncle Augustus would tire of carrying it and realize he needed to take the antidote. There was also the little matter of keeping the book stocked. "How will you get enough insects to be satisfied?"

"Watch." Uncle darted out through the French doors.

While we waited for Uncle to return, I tried to catch Professor Lepworthy's attention to tell him what I thought of his scheme, but he refused to meet my gaze and hummed tunelessly as he stared off into space. Less than thirty seconds later, my avuncular relation was back.

The professor set out several bits of waxed paper. As Uncle Augustus placed an insect on each piece, the professor folded the paper and stuck it into the book. When the two of them were finished, quite a few slips of paper protruded from between the pages.

Uncle Augustus stepped back and surveyed his work. "Very good. Very good, indeed." Sliding one of the pieces of waxed paper from the book, he plucked out the enclosed flattened insect and crunched contentedly. Then he repeated the action so quickly that if I had not known what he was doing, I would have been unable to tell what had happened. He turned to me. "See, Petronella? I think we'll be all right."

He looked so happy, I didn't have the heart to protest. "Very well, Uncle. We'll see how it goes." In spite of what I said, though, I didn't like the situation at all and could only hope he would see his way to taking the antidote soon.

Chapter Seven

In Which Luggage Portends Ominous Tidings

WHEN ONE'S NEAREST AND DEAREST is trying one's patience beyond bearing, it does not do one's patience the least bit of good to be forcefully thrust into the presence of additional trying relations, especially when one has not slept at all well. Such was my thought upon descending the stairs later that morning and being presented with the horrifying sight of luggage. Luggage in itself is innocuous enough. However, luggage sitting in the entrance hall unannounced portends ominous tidings.

At that moment Moriarty, my butler, glided across the hall carrying a covered tray. Moriarty always glides as if on roller skates in a manner that has fascinated me since I was a child. While still in the nursery, I often tried to mimic him, without success. I evidently do not possess the same musculature as my esteemed butler. I'm not sure any other human being does, except one, and I preferred not to think about my great-aunt Theophilia under any circumstances.

As Moriarty neatly circumvented the pile of luggage, I cleared my throat. He paused in midglide and looked up at me inquiringly. "Yes, Miss Arbuthnot?"

"To whom does the luggage belong?"

Moriarty permitted himself a small smile. "Why, to Lady Farworthy and Mr. Cyril, Miss Arbuthnot."

I staggered and would have tumbled down the stairs had I not sunk down to sit on the stair just behind me. Oh, dear. Aunt Cordelia and her odious son Cyril. Nothing could be worse.

"Are you quite all right, Miss Arbuthnot? You are looking a bit peaked." Moriarty glided up the stairs and whipped out his treasured vial of smelling salts.

I jumped to a standing position before he could open the bottle. As long as I have known him, he has carried the thing in his pocket, waiting to afflict with its pungent aroma any poor fainting female who happened to be within his vicinity. The salts were of his own concocting, and one sniff of the vial's contents was guaranteed to bring one into a most startled upright position unless one were already deceased, and even then the effect might be equally salubrious. Jane and I called it the Vile Vial.

"Petronella?" a stentorian voice brayed from the direction of the drawing room.

My eyes rolled toward the ceiling of their own accord, and a shiver of apprehension ran through me. How would I ever explain Uncle Augustus to Aunt Cordelia, who was my father's next older sibling and had never approved of my mother's relations? I straightened my shoulders as much as I could and entered the drawing room only to be met by a sight that drained what little starch there was left in me out through my toes. Aunt Cordelia stood chest out, her khaki explorer shirt and skirt pressed, and her monocle firmly screwed into place. She would have been altogether intimidating if not for her absurd affinity for golden ringlets, which hung from beneath her pith helmet. I'd always wondered if those ringlets were her own hair, but I had never seen her without the pith helmet and so could not say.

"Well?" said Aunt.

Cyril sniggered.

I shot him a look that he well understood. It said I would deal with him later, and I knew that if he remembered the incident of the pickled herrings, he knew that I could, too. Evidently he did, because the sniggering stopped in mid-snig.

"Well, what, dear Aunt Cordelia?" I asked mildly, and smiled as a young girl should smile at an aunt she has not seen in over a year—an aunt renowned for carrying on the Arbuthnot tradition of intrepid adventuring.

Aunt Cordelia screwed the monocle in tighter and harrumphed a bit. "I leave for a mere few months of pleasant exploration in the jungles of Burma, and you not only decide to have your coming-out party without me, but you get yourself into a pickle." She shot the last word out in such a manner that if it had been a real pickle, she would have skewered me with it. I wondered if, after all, she knew of the pickled herrings, although I doubted that Cyril would have had the fortitude to tell his dear *mama*. In my opinion, Cyril was a disgrace to the Arbuthnot name, much more like his cowed *papa* over whom Aunt Cordelia ruled from under her pith helmet.

Aunt Cordelia waved a copy of the *Times* toward me as if its existence amply explained her perturbation. I caught a glimpse of the words *Dame* and *Generalissimo* on the front page.

I was saved the necessity of answering, for at that moment the front door slammed open. Moriarty sailed from the room only to return moments later, barely keeping up with the only other person I knew who could outglide my butler—my great-aunt Theophilia, who was my father's aunt, although she was about his age. She was also the only person I knew who could cow Aunt Cordelia, and in truth my esteemed and ringleted aunt seemed nearly as taken aback as I was. One aunt was more than I could bear, but two presented one with enough reason to consider the murky depths of the Thames as a pleasant resting place for one's remains.

Had it not been for Uncle Augustus's fortitude some years earlier, my aunts would have been in control of my considerable fortune. Since then, they had sought every opportunity to prove Uncle unfit as my guardian. I shuddered to think what they would do if they understood his present condition.

Moriarty managed to maneuver himself in front of Great-aunt Theophilia so he could stand to attention and announce, "Her excellency, the Duchess of Worffingdon, and her daughters Lady Crimea and Miss Boeotia."

Crimea and Boeotia stepped into full view, dressed to the nines in the latest tailored traveling suits and large, fruit-decorated hats. Crimea, older than I by a year, and Boeotia, a deceptively golden-haired, apple-cheeked child of six, smiled at me. I was sharply reminded of Great-aunt Theophilia's and Great-uncle Hevrington's practice of naming their children after places where he had served while in the military. Fortunately, they had never produced a third child. Great-uncle Hevrington's last stint had been in Famagusta.

"Hello, dear cousin," said Crimea in a manner that let me know she remembered the incident of the pig's tail in much the same manner Cyril remembered the incident of the pickled herrings.

I nodded and smiled, albeit querulously.

Two unpleasant aunts and three atrocious cousins. If the Thames had conveniently flowed past my veranda, I would gladly have tossed myself in. A glance toward that sunny porch just beyond the French windows confirmed my suspicion that it was Thames-less. However, it produced the alarming sight of Uncle Augustus toe-teetering on the rail while reaching toward the heavens with a butterfly net. I was further shocked to see practically all of my serving and underserving staff similarly fitted out with nets and flitting about the lawn. Thank the heavens above that I was positioned at the opposite end of the drawing room and my relations were all facing me.

"Well?" said Great-aunt Theophilia in a richer echo of Aunt Cordelia's earlier greeting. Her lustrous curls peeked from underneath a hat that was the height of fashion, being made of a vast array of feathers and silk flowers. The hat, combined with her tailored traveling dress and exquisite figure, made Aunt Cordelia's getup fall from a state of intimidation to a state of gracelessness. In fact, my younger aunt looked rather wilted.

The jellification of Aunt Cordelia's spine served to stiffen mine. Quite cordially I said, "What a pleasant surprise to have so many of my dear ones restored to British shores so suddenly. I had word that you, Aunt Theophilia, and Crimea and Boeotia were shopping in Paris, while you, Aunt Cordelia, were, as you mentioned, in the jungles of Burma. Otherwise you most assuredly would have been invited to the party my uncle Augustus gave for my coming out."

Great-aunt Theophilia raised a lorgnette to examine me much like Professor Lepworthy might have examined one of his entomological specimens. I immediately decided that lorgnettes are more effective than monocles for giving one a superior air. Perhaps I should have to affect one when I was older and wished to intimidate relations.

"Indeed" was all she said.

I knew what she was up to with her one-word stratagems. She was endeavoring to induce me to babble. Well, she would soon find I had more of the Arbuthnot in me than that, and some Percival as well.

"Indeed," I answered and managed not to wince as I observed Uncle Augustus leap weightlessly from the rail and out of sight.

However, the necessity of refusing to babble was taken out of my hands as Moriarty glided into the room, a silver tray presented on his upturned hand. He stopped before me. On the silver tray was a note on which lay another squashed Tou-eh-mah-mah Island butterfly.

Chapter Eight

In Which the Drawing Room
Becomes Crowded

OUR COLLECTIVE GAZE WAS FIXED on the Tou-eh-mah-mah butterfly much as the butterfly was affixed to the note.

There are moments when all motion is slowed so that a split second seems stretched out to a lifetime. Such interludes allow one to contemplate the meaning of life and perhaps to absorb enough of the entailing circumstances so that one may make wiser decisions than would otherwise be possible.

This was not one of those moments.

Great-aunt Theophilia lost her dignity enough to lunge toward the tray, hand outstretched. However, she clasped only Aunt Cordelia's fingers, which clutched empty air because Moriarty had moved the silver tray just enough in my direction so that I could snatch the note myself. I would have sworn Moriarty winked at me as he did so, but I discounted such a gesture as beyond my stoic butler's capabilities.

"Well," said Great-aunt Theophilia as she drew herself back and up to her former grand state.

"Hmmph," said Aunt Cordelia.

"Just read it, for goodness' sake," said Boeotia.

At that moment Uncle Augustus strolled in, impeccably turned out and looking strangely scholarly with an extremely large book under one arm that I recognized as *Insectile Creatures*. The tome had many more bits of waxed paper sticking out of its pages than had been there earlier, making the book bulge. What did Uncle Augustus think he was doing? The last people I wanted to know of his unfortunate condition were my paternal relatives.

Before I could react, Uncle Augustus's hand shot forth in a blur and snatched the note from my fingers. In fact, he was so precipitate in his actions I'm quite certain neither Great-aunt Theophilia nor Aunt Cordelia, nor any other of my esteemed relations, registered more than the fact that the note suddenly appeared in Uncle's hand. I began to protest, remembering his previous experience with a Tou-eh-mah-mah butterfly affixed to a note, but he merely smiled reassuringly in my direction, cleared his throat, and patted the book under his arm meaningfully. He opened his mouth to speak, only to be interrupted by Boeotia.

"Are you going to read the note or not? I'm simply dying to know what is in it." Her comment was greeted by a murmur of agreement from around the room. The fact that Great-aunt Theophilia did not chide her daughter for such rude behavior is evidence of the level of anticipation we all labored under.

Uncle unfolded the note. Everyone inhaled in expectation.

"Lord Sinclair and Miss Jane Sinclair," announced Moriarty.

Everyone exhaled.

Jane and James stepped into the room. Jane appeared much refreshed after her night's rest, especially since she was wearing a dainty rose blush shirtwaist and skirt, white stockings, and heeled white strappy pumps. James, of course, outshone even Uncle in sartorial splendor. He certainly made Cyril appear frumpish by comparison. I noticed that James's jacket sat exceptionally well on his broad shoulders. With some difficulty I pulled my gaze from his well-muscled shoulders to Jane's smiling face.

"Jane, darling, and James. Do come in. Uncle is about to read another note that has just arrived, we think, from the kidnappers."

"Another note?" said James as Jane leaned forward and kissed my cheek in greeting. Being greeted with a kiss by one's greatest friend is a pleasant experience, but I must

53

admit a kiss from her brother would have been even more welcome. Alas, none was forthcoming.

Jane said, "And we have interrupted. We're so sorry. Please continue, Mr. Percival."

"He hadn't even started," said Boeotia in disgust.

"But I shall now," said Uncle Augustus. He held the note up to read. "To—"

"Inspector Higginbotham and Sergeant Crumple," announced Moriarty.

"Good morning, Miss Arbuthnot," said Inspector Higginbotham, a trifle too unctuously for my liking. His manner made me suspect something, although I could not imagine what.

"Good morning, Inspector. Sergeant Crumple," I said. "We were about to—"

"Read it!" shouted Boeotia.

"I am about to," said Uncle.

"Mr. George Grimsley," announced Moriarty.

"Ahhh!" screamed Boeotia.

Chapter Nine

In Which the Messenger Eats Chocolates

IN DEALING WITH ONE'S RELATIONS, one is often reminded of the maxim "There is many a slip 'twixt the cup and the lip." The wisdom of that saying was especially apparent in these circumstances. When one adds one's relations to the mix of kidnappers, notes, friends, acquaintances, and inspectors from Scotland Yard, one must expect the worst or fall victim to the most unseemly surprises, such as my impatient relations converging on Uncle Augustus and attempting to grab the note from his grasp before he could read it. Fortunately, Uncle's newly developed physical abilities enabled him to leap from their midst and victoriously carry off the scrap of paper to the stairs in the front hall, where he read:

Miss Arbuthnot,

You will bring twenty thousand pounds British sterling to Nelson's Column at midnight tonight. Deposit it under the death scene. Do not fail, or the dame and generalissimo will perish just as Nelson did. Come alone.

The note seemed straightforward enough, although the phrasing was a bit confusing. Did the kidnappers mean that the dame and generalissimo would die in the manner that Nelson had died, or that Nelson had died and so would the generalissimo and dame? My former governess Miss Spackering would have taken the writer to task for lack of clarity. However, I was more interested in the message itself.

A number of thoughts flitted through my mind, just as Uncle flitted through the shrubberies: The dame and generalissimo were alive. I hoped Parliament saw fit to fork over the twenty thousand pounds. The abductors had atrocious penmanship, which matched their grasp of grammar. Who had brought that note? And finally, James's tailor truly had done a superb job of fitting his jacket across his muscular shoulders.

At that moment a roar erupted from my relations and the Yard personnel as they stood at the base of the staircase vying for Uncle Augustus's attention. I, on the other hand, signaled Moriarty to meet me by the front door. Then I caught the attention of Jane and James and motioned to them to join us.

"Yes, miss?" asked my butler.

"Where is the messenger who delivered the note?"

"Anticipating such a question, I took the liberty of apprehending the young person. He is in the care of Thomas the gardener and several undergardeners in the arboretum, awaiting questioning, miss."

"Excellent." My friends and I were halfway out the door when Moriarty presented me with a large gold foil box of chocolates in the shape of a heart. Uncle Augustus had given it to me as a birthday gift. Fortunately, Uncle had chosen it before his unfortunate episode with the beetle; therefore it was from one of the finest chocolatiers in London.

Moriarty explained, "Excuse me, miss, but it occurs to me that the young messenger might be more persuaded to divulge information if he were sweetened up, as it were, by chocolates administered at propitious moments, rather than by threats."

"Do you mean that we're to bribe him?" asked James, on the verge of outrage.

"Naturally," I said as I tucked the gold box under my arm. "And if chocolates aren't enough, I intend to try money."

"Or tears," said Jane. "Tears work quite well on most males. Even you, dearest brother. This is, after all, a crisis of international consequence and requires the utmost diplomacy."

As Jane and I strode in the direction of the arboretum, I heard James mutter, "I'm not sure chocolates and tears are among the Home Office–approved methods of interrogation."

Jane and I ignored James's comment as being unworthy of reply. The male of the species can be astonishingly out of touch with reality at times.

The sight that met my eyes when we arrived at the arboretum was a pitiful one indeed. Thomas the gardener and his minions stood around a small, tearful, uniformed boy. I recognized the uniform as belonging to the messenger service in the nearest town—Upper Middle Totley-on-Wode.

I dropped to one knee in front of the boy in order to be at eye level and said, "Thank you for bringing the message. What's your name?" I opened the box of chocolates.

The boy's attention was immediately caught by the brilliantly colored foil-wrapped candies amid other tempting chocolates in little cups. "Ralph," he answered with a sniff. Before he could rub his nose on his sleeve, James thrust a white handkerchief into the urchin's hand, and Ralph obediently wiped his nose, although his attention remained on the chocolates.

"Ralph. That's a nice name." I offered a milk chocolate crème to the little fellow, who immediately stuffed it into his mouth before eyeing the rest of the candy. I held a chocolate-covered caramel just out of his reach. "Who gave you the message to deliver to me?"

Ralph's fingers stretched toward the chocolate. "Don't know him."

"Was it someone in the messenger office?"

"Naw."

"So you were not given the message at the office. Where did you get the message?" I waved the caramel a bit to keep his attention on it.

"Foreign bloke at the train station." He snatched the caramel and popped it into his mouth.

Jane proffered a butter crème. "Was he a foreign gentle-man with a blond goatee, a wart on his nose, a plaid um-brella, and a high, squeaky voice?"

The boy rolled his eyes and laughed at Jane's ridiculous description, his mood evidently much improved by the choc-olate. "Not likely. More like a black mustache and slouch hat. 'Is voice weren't real high, neither—kind of breathy-like, though you were dead on 'bout the wart. But it were 'is boots what caught me eye. They was mucky, wif pretty bugs on 'em like this one 'ere." He reached into his uniform pocket and produced a Tou-eh-mah-mah butterfly, quite dead and rather squashed, but with the "Phui" still plainly inscribed on its wings.

When I reached for it, Ralph held it away until I popped a cherry cordial chocolate into his mouth. Then, to my surprise, the butterfly was lifted from my hand by Uncle Augustus. I had not heard him approach. His new physical prowess was quite extraordinary. Uncle usually galumphed like an elephant.

"Well, niece, what do we have here?"

"Don't eat it!" My protest died on my lips as I rose to my feet. Everyone but Uncle, James, and Jane looked at me oddly.

Rather than eating the insect, Uncle extracted a slip of waxed paper from *Insectile Creatures*, which he still carried. Then he folded the paper over the butterfly and deposited it between the pages of the book, where several other bits of paper enveloping insects were still ensconced.

"Sir," said one of the undergardeners as he stepped forward holding out his hat, in which I could see the flash of brilliant purple wings. "I caught one just like it near the woods."

"Petronella!" I heard Great-aunt Theophilia call as she picked her elegant way across the lawn. "What do you have there? Why are you all out here?" Behind her trailed Crimea, Boeotia, and Georgie Grimsley in conversation with Cyril, and behind them came Inspector Higginbotham and Sergeant Crumple.

Aunt Cordelia matched Theophilia step for step. "Really, Petronella. You do make it difficult to protect you in these dangerous circumstances. If I were your guardian, I would keep you safely in the house," she shouted.

"Luckily she isn't your guardian," whispered Jane in my ear.

"Right, but she'd like to be in charge of my fortune. The last thing I need is that horde following me about," I whispered back. I turned to the undergardener. "In which part of the woods did you find the butterfly?"

"Over there, miss."

Hoping to escape my inveterate relatives and other investigators, I headed in the direction he indicated, only to see the horde moving to intercept me. I changed course and so did they, following me rather like the tail of a comet, strung out as they were. I sighed. Evidently, everyone was determined to follow me no matter which way I went.

Feeling safer among friends, I returned to my place near Ralph, who looked expectantly at my chocolate box. Then I noticed that Thomas the gardener and his staff were also looking expectantly at the box. An idea formed in my head.

"Let's all search the woods. Anyone who finds more of

these butterflies or any clues as to where they come from will get chocolates," I said.

Thomas and his staff took off at a run.

I held Ralph by the hand and asked, "Kind sir, would you be so good as to accompany me? I have some more questions to ask you."

He nodded.

"Are you inviting us as well?" asked James. I noticed that the morning sunshine glistened on his brilliantined locks and brought into relief his excessively handsome physiognomy.

"With all my heart," I said before I could stop myself. Then I bent to offer Ralph a chocolate, hoping to hide the resulting blush.

"Petronella!" my aunts cried in unison. They were nearly upon us.

Uncle glanced at the approaching horde with something like panic on his face. "Follow me. I have an idea."

My small band of conspirators and I scrambled after Uncle Augustus as he headed off in a slightly different direction from the gardeners. A glance over my shoulder told me that the horde veered in his direction right behind us. Were we never to be rid of them? Probably not until they found some reason to depose Uncle as the guardian of my fortune. I could only hope that once we were in the woods we could give them the slip.

Chapter Ten

In Which Logs Are Not Inspected

I SOON REALIZED TO MY dismay that one's carefully acquired sense of fashion, meant to assist one while navigating the jungles of polite society, has little worth when navigating the woods of one's estate. Sleuthing requires a more appropriate wardrobe than ruched shirtwaists with lace insets, S-bend corsets, and high-heeled pumps—the corset especially made it difficult to breathe deeply. As I stepped over fallen branches and disengaged my delicate voile and lace skirts from brambles, I found myself coveting Aunt Cordelia's khakis, something I heretofore had not thought possible.

Additionally, I could only suppose that Uncle led us this way because he had explored it during his predations on winged and multilegged creatures the previous night. I was also dismayed to hear the sound of my esteemed relations crashing through the woods behind us.

"Where're we going and whotcher want to know? I got to get back to the message office or Mr. Smiff will have me 'ead," complained Ralph, evidently suffering from a belated case of work ethic.

Puffing slightly from the exertion of clambering over a fallen tree — although I might also have been a bit breathless because James had helped me — I asked Ralph, "Was the foreign gentleman at the train station waiting for a train, or had he just arrived?"

Ralph screwed up his face in an apparent effort to think, while James helped Jane over the fallen log. We had reached a clearing and could just see Uncle Augustus disappearing along the path ahead of us. Our way now unimpeded, we sped up, trying to catch up with my dear uncle.

Ralph ignored the proffered box of chocolates and said, "He were looking at the train schedule to London when he saw me give a message to the station master and asked me to deliver the one I brung to you. He give me a shilling, too. None of them tuppence."

I could see that the charm of chocolates as a bribe was beginning to wane.

James, evidently having been converted to expediency, held two shillings out to the young opportunist, who snatched them as soon as they appeared. "Those shillings are for you and another one besides if you can remember anything else about the man in the slouch hat. Was he short or tall? Did he say anything else? Did you see him get on the train? Which one?"

"Short. Got on the London 9:23. Muttered to himself in some heathen foreign tongue. Only fing I caught was somefing like *salas.*" Ralph held out his hand for the other shilling.

James looked both startled and thoughtful as he handed the coin to the boy. "*Salas.* I wonder."

Ralph saluted us and sprinted off in what I knew to be the direction of Upper Middle Totley-on-Wode. I remembered that the message office was just down the street from the train station, which made Ralph's information all the more credible.

I did not have time to ask James what he wondered. We'd arrived at the end of the path, and my aunts were right behind us. Aunt Cordelia, who had not been encumbered by fashion, was in the lead. The path opened onto a lane that ran along the borders of a meadow. I recognized it as belonging to the Barrowspring Farm, leased from me by Farmer Hodgkins, as generations of his ancestors had leased it from my ancestors. The meadow was inhabited by a large bull that had chased me not three years ago when I tweaked

65

its tail. It had been a dangerous and foolish thing to do, but I was, after all, an Arbuthnot and a Percival, and had begun an early career of adventures. The lane also ran close to the shrubberies that edged the large lawn where my coming-out party had taken place. Things were starting to fall into place.

"Petronella," panted Aunt Cordelia, her golden ringlets bouncing from beneath her pith helmet with each breath. However, she could not seem to find the energy to say more.

Not so Great-aunt Theophilia as she glided into the lane, looking almost as neatly attired as she had in my drawing room. I could not say the same for Crimea and Boeotia, who shot me looks of immense dislike as they tried to smooth their skirts and straighten their hats. Crimea's, with its bunches of fruit amid feathers, was especially askew and, I might add, ridiculous.

Great-aunt Theophilia said, "Petronella. You look a disgrace and your behavior is reprehensible. If your uncle is encouraging you in—"

"Doing her duty to God and king?" interrupted Uncle Augustus.

"Well," breathed Great-aunt Theophilia.

Uncle took my arm and steered me down the lane to where a tumble of logs blocked part of the road. Over his shoulder, he called, "Inspector, if you need to inspect something, then inspect these logs, if you please."

Inspector Higginbotham, brushing leaves from his tweed jacket and followed by Sergeant Crumple, headed for the logs. "And what do we have here? It looks like a pile of logs, if you ask me."

"Yes, sir. That it do," said Crumple. I noticed that one of his packing-twine shoelaces was broken.

Uncle Augustus's face took on the studiously patient expression of one dealing with persons of less than normal levels of wit. "Yes, I do admit they are logs, but I do not recall seeing logs like these before. How did they get here? Where did they come from? They could be a clue."

I agreed with Uncle. The logs had cinnamon-colored bark that hung in long strips between patches of brilliant green lichen. Sunning themselves on the pile were two Toueh-mah-mah butterflies, their purple, yellow, and turquoise wings illuminated against the dark bark. Suddenly something large and cartilaginous pounced on one of the butterflies and began devouring it with a gusto that rivaled Uncle Augustus's. It was a beetle like the one Uncle had swallowed, but so much larger that it would have been difficult even for Uncle to ingest this creature in one bite.

"I say. I wonder if Maximus knows that the beetles feed on the butterflies," said Uncle, more to himself than to anyone in particular, his hands clasped tightly around *Insectile Creatures*. I was grateful that he was restraining himself from feasting in front of my aunts.

"Here is something of real interest," said Inspector Higginbotham, who had wandered down the lane a few feet. All of us converged on him. He waved us back. "Now don't destroy the evidence. Look at the wagon ruts. Not so unusual for a country lane, correct? But look at what I found in one of the ruts." He reached down and then held out his hand, palm up, to display a glittering ruby. "The generalissimo had rubies in his medals. Am I correct?"

Uncle, James, Jane, and I nodded.

Uncle pointed to the ruts, which we all studied obediently. "Excellent clue, Inspector. Notice how the impressions stop just where you found the ruby, and the ground next to them is scuffed with footprints. It is possible that a wagon was stopped here, the logs were unloaded, and the generalissimo and dame were loaded into it and transported away."

We all turned toward the inspector to see what he thought of Uncle's brilliant deduction.

The inspector shrugged, his attention trained on the ruby in his hand. "Perhaps. It's of no consequence how they were transported. What is important is that the ruby establishes the presence of the victims at this spot. I must report our findings to my superiors and see what can be done about the ransom."

"But what about me? I'm supposed to deliver it," I said.

The inspector ignored my comment as both he and Sergeant Crumple stumped off in the direction of Upper Middle Totley-on-Wode in order to take the train to London and the Yard.

I almost called them back, since I felt somewhat responsible for the kidnappings. Then I decided that they obviously did not feel I was responsible for anything, which was a bit disheartening.

"Well," huffed Great-aunt Theophilia. It appeared to be her favorite expression today. She seemed about to say something else, but at that moment further crashings in the woods caused us to turn in that direction. One of the undergardeners, followed by Thomas and the others of his staff, stumbled out into the lane. When they saw us, they nearly fell over each other in their hurry to reach us, making Crimea and Boeotia jump back in alarm.

"Miss! Miss! We didn't find more butterflies, but we did find these." Into my hand the undergardener placed a glittering, although bent, tiara that I recognized as having been worn by Dame Carruthers on the night of her doom and a coin that I didn't recognize at all.

"What kind of coin is this?" I held it up to the sunlight to read the inscription. "Why, this is a Colombian coin. It says it is a *peso*," I exclaimed.

"Is it worth a chocolate, anyway?" asked the under-gardener.

Chapter Eleven

In Which a Diversion Is Discerned

WHEN ONE HAS BEEN THE center of attention for a considerable amount of time, to be treated as inconsequential, as the inspector had treated me, has the effect of bringing one rather low. Was it possible that I was not as clever as I had been led to believe? Perhaps I was no better than Georgie Grimsley—perish the thought—who was chattering with Cyril. It turned out that they were schoolmates. I hoped Georgie did not feel that Cyril's visit gave him an excuse to grace us with his presence on a continual basis.

"Here now," said Jane, slipping her arm through mine as we walked back to the house. "That inspector obviously has an overinflated sense of his own worth. He will find to his sorrow that he should have listened more carefully to you and your uncle."

James joined us. "What pomposity. I'm afraid that inspector reminds me all too much of certain people I know in government."

I smiled at my friends, my heart eased by their comments, even as it palpitated quickly at having James so near. "We do have some rather interesting clues that he took no notice of, do we not?" I asked.

Back in my drawing room, the remaining horde soon set to feasting upon the crumpets, tea cakes, and tea that I had asked Moriarty to supply. While James, Jane, and I ate—and Uncle snacked surreptitiously—we sat at the far end of the table and examined our collection of clues.

Besides serving us lunch, Moriarty had also been good enough to acquire several glass jars with stout lids, which we arranged on the table. In the jars we placed the beetle, the remaining butterfly, and strips of bark from the logs, to which were attached chrysalises. We rather hoped that more butterflies might hatch. The beetle could obviously see the butterfly in the container next to it because it kept throwing itself against the side of its bottle, just as Uncle had thrown himself against the glass cases in Professor Lepworthy's office.

Next to the bottles we also laid the Colombian *peso* and the bent tiara and a scrap of paper on which was written the word *ruby*. Altogether we had accumulated a fair number of interesting items, but I failed to see how they could lead us to the dame and generalissimo.

From her Italian leather handbag, Jane produced a small pad of paper and a pencil. "Perhaps we should make a list of what we know about the case."

"Tip-top idea, old flesh and blood," said James. "We should put them into categories—one category per page. First two, of course, should be Dame Carruthers and the generalissimo."

Getting into the spirit of things, I said, "Another page could be the man who gave Ralph the message."

"And another could be the wagon. Transportation is important, in spite of what the inspector thinks," added Uncle Augustus.

When we had finished adding items to our lists, we surveyed the pages laid out on the table in front of the bottles.

"Have you noticed how the majority of the clues are related to Colombia and Panama?" I said. "It would seem that, other than Dame Carruthers, everything hinges on those two countries."

"Although Dame Carruthers does appear to be important as leverage to get the twenty thousand pounds," said Jane.

James smacked his forehead with his palm, nearly propelling his hirsute splendor into oblivion. "Of course! It's staring us in the face, and we never saw it."

"It?" I hissed, trying not to attract the attention of my relations or Georgie Grimsley, who, I deduced from the way he kept smirking at me, was flirting outrageously with Crimea in order to pay me back for ignoring him. Poor girl. Georgie Grimsley's attentions were a heavy price to pay for interfering uninvited in international relations.

"Yes, what do you mean?" asked Uncle Augustus. "Are you privy to some information from the Home Office that pertains to this case? Can you tell us?"

"Perhaps I can. It's really no secret," said James thoughtfully.

"It?" hissed Jane and I in unison. I was suddenly in sympathy with Miss Spackering, my former governess, for insisting on clarity regarding pronoun referents.

"The kidnapping is a diversion. At least I think it is." James grinned at our shocked and outraged expressions. "Although we know the Colombians are probably happy to have Generalissimo Reyes-Cardoza in their clutches, there is more at stake now than capturing a rebel officer."

Light dawned. "Of course—the canal and all. So why do they need a diversion?"

"Britain is siding with the Americans, of course, because we need the canal. One of the communiqués I saw from the Colombian ambassador threatened retribution if we don't change our policy."

"But what could a poor nation such as Colombia do to Britain?" asked Jane.

"I'm not sure, but if we are concentrating our national attentions on finding Dame Carruthers and Generalissimo Reyes-Cardoza, they may be able to put something in place while we aren't looking."

"It makes sense," I said. "If they wanted to do serious damage, they would have asked for more than twenty thousand pounds. Such a sum would hardly impoverish Britain."

"The question is, how can we stop them?" said James.

"No one will believe us unless we have more evidence," said Jane.

James stroked his manly chin thoughtfully. "If only we knew more about the man who gave Ralph the message. Then I would have something concrete to report to my superiors."

A half-formed plan popped into my head. I consulted my watch and then caught Moriarty's eye and nodded. When he came over, I said quietly, "Please have Bumbridge bring the carriage around. We'll be going to the train station."

Now it was James's turn to look puzzled. "What?"

"Shh," I warned. "We will leave this room one at a time and go in different directions so we do not attract the attention of the relatives, and then meet outside the front door.

The same train that took the Colombian to London has had time to get there and come back and be ready to go to London again. Jane and I used to escape from our governesses for a few hours by riding back and forth on that train, so we know the schedule. We can search the cars for more clues as we ride."

Chapter Twelve

In Which an Eye Is Blackened

AS I SLIPPED OUT THE servants' entrance and around to the front where Bumbridge—almost as fine an example of efficiency as Moriarty—waited with the carriage, I mused that nothing I'd ever experienced in my short life was as exhilarating as escape. Miss Spackering had been a praiseworthy and astute governess, but she was no match for my Arbuthnot- and Percival-bred skills at evasion—skills I had employed in my childhood with regularity and success. I often thought fondly of an ancestor I strove to emulate who had not only managed to escape from Cromwell's forces, but had also ingeniously freed himself from the Tower of London when the Royalists returned to power and imprisoned him because of a misunderstanding. They later apologized when he rode into London with his personal army.

With my good humor restored, I accepted my hat, my Italian gloves, and my favorite French crewel-embroidered handbag from the ever-thoughtful Moriarty, who handed me up into the carriage. There I found Uncle snacking on delicacies previously hidden in *Insectile Creatures*. At least he was doing so in privacy. I pretended not to notice as I placed the tiara and *peso* into my handbag. We were joined by Jane and then, soon after, by James.

James puffed a bit as he entered the carriage. He mopped at his brow with another of his snowy handkerchiefs. "I say, your pith-helmeted aunt gave a good account of herself while chasing me through the kitchen. I barely managed to give her the slip by detouring through the dairy."

Just as the carriage horses accelerated into a trot, I heard a faint "Petronella!" Through the carriage window I viewed Aunt Cordelia vigorously brandishing an umbrella on the front steps. Bumbridge, efficient as ever, cracked his whip and the horses broke into a canter. I settled back against the squabs, satisfied that we would not be followed for quite some time. According to my watch and what I knew of the train schedule, we should be pulling out before any of the horde could reach the station.

"Do you really think there will be any clues on the train?" asked Jane.

"It's entirely possible, old stick," said James. "After all, Ralph did say the fellow's shoes were mucky, and I don't expect the railroad will have had time to clean the floors yet."

"We may also get some information from the station-master. He might know where the Colombian intended to leave the train. Then we could ask people at that stop if they have seen him," I said, trying to ignore the crunching coming from Uncle's corner, next to me.

"Capital idea!" exclaimed James. Then his magnificent brow darkened. "But I shall do the asking. It is all very well for the two of you to collect clues in the safety of the country-side, but quite another matter for you to brave the dangers of the unsavory side of London."

Jane and I did not deign to answer him. We merely glanced at each other, one eyebrow raised. If James only knew of some of the escapades his exemplary sister and I had experienced in the safety of the countryside, he might not be so complacent about our going into London, after all. I was reminded especially of the time Jane and I had loosed a large number of garden snakes among the participants in the village sack race. The resulting race times were admirable, although the number of people who saw the end of the race was much diminished from what it had been at the beginning. I do not believe that the record set that day has been bested since.

The carriage slowed enough for me to hear the familiar midday village sounds of Upper Middle Totley-on-Wode. Just as I had predicted, a train rested in front of the station, with clouds of steam rising, pointed in the direction of London. We ascended the platform, where the stationmaster rushed to greet us.

"Why, Miss Arbuthnot. Mr. Percival. Lord Sinclair. Miss Sinclair. What can I do for you?"

"Hello, Mr. Drake. Do you recall a foreign gentleman in a slouch hat who bought a ticket to London this morning?" asked James.

"Very well. Don't get many foreigners in these parts."

"Then you'd remember where he was going?"

"Bought a ticket to Charing Cross Station, he did."

James produced some money. "Thank you. We'd like four tickets to Charing Cross Station."

The train was mostly empty, as was normal for a midday run to London, so we had our choice of compartments and ample opportunity to search.

Since we had chosen a compartment in the middle of the train, I said to Jane, "Would it be all right if Uncle and I search from here to the rear of the train, and would you and James search the front?"

"Certainly," said Jane, and James nodded agreement.

I would have enjoyed having James as my partner no end, or even Jane, but I also felt responsible for Uncle's safety and decorum. The last part of the train it would have to be, since I had to be my Uncle's warden. At least, the rear of the train was usually more sparsely occupied, so there would be less chance for him to publicly misbehave.

After searching three compartments, one thing became profoundly clear — British trains are by no means insect free. Uncle and I did not find remnants of Tou-eh-mah-mah butterflies or beetles, but we did find a surfeit of spiders, flies, ants, and all sorts of other insects. I concluded that I would never be able to travel in public transport again without checking corners and crevices. In one compartment, in particular, a large number of ants that were blithely feasting on the remnants of someone's sack lunch became picnic fare for Uncle.

The next two compartments produced nothing more interesting than additional prospective sustenance for Uncle and a morning London newspaper. However, when I stepped from the rear platform of our carriage into the next, I was surprised to find a disheveled and sweaty Georgie Grimsley.

"Why, Mr. Grimsley. Whatever are you doing here?" I asked as I circled around the young man and peered into the first compartment.

"Didn't know I had a bicycle, did you?" he said. "Thought you'd get away."

"Get away? I don't understand your meaning." I lifted a newspaper from the floor and shook it out. Nothing fell. I moved on to the next compartment, while Uncle searched the seat cushions for sustenance.

Georgie Grimsley followed me. "You and your smarmy friends thought you could ditch me."

"Ditch? Where do you come up with such words? You must be mistaken." My reply was made in an inattentive fashion because I had spotted another Colombian *peso* resting on the seat just where a trouser pocket would have deposited its contents. As I reached for the coin, however, Georgie Grimsley snatched it from beneath my fingers.

I sighed. Really, he was being too tiresome. "Mr. Grimsley. Would you be so kind as to hand me that coin?"

"Not until you look at me. You always ignore me."

I looked at him. It was not a pretty sight, especially his overlong nose hairs. "Now, please give me the coin." I held out my hand and was appalled to have him grab it and hold on. "Mr. Grimsley. My hand and the coin, please."

"Petronella, Pet. I may call you Pet, mayn't I?"

"No, you most certainly may not."

He pulled me closer. "You know I have loved you since I first set eyes on you. If we change trains in London, we can

82

make it to Gretna Green in a few hours and be married. I know you'd like that."

I struggled to disengage myself. The little fiend had a grip like a vise. "Is this about your impecunious family's debts? Much good marrying me will do you. I must tell you that I don't come into the majority of my inheritance until I'm twenty-one. Besides, I heard that you proposed to Jessalyn St. John last week."

"How can you speak of money when I'm declaring my undying devotion?" he cried as he grabbed my other hand.

At that moment, the train swayed and I was able to free one hand. Fortunately, that hand clasped the strap of my French crewel-embroidered handbag, which struck Georgie Grimsley in the eye with a satisfactory *thwop!*

I was immediately released.

"Ow! Ow! and I say ow again!" Clutching his eye, Georgie stumbled backward and flopped onto the seat, where he writhed rather like one of the earthworms Uncle had plucked from among the rocks in my garden.

While he gyrated, I decided that discretion was the better part of valor and fled back to the train car where I had left Uncle Augustus. I was followed by Georgie Grimsley's wailing, "You'll be sorry for this. I swear you will!"

Chapter Thirteen

In Which Sticky Buns Are Devoured

AS I SCUTTLED BACK TO Uncle, I reflected with growing indignation that one's first proposal of marriage should be memorable because of pleasant associations, rather than sweaty hands and struggles with a repugnant philanderer. I was so intent on retribution that when Uncle Augustus abruptly emerged from a compartment, we collided.

"There you are," he said, stuffing a bit of waxed paper into *Insectile Creatures*.

"Oh, Uncle. I was nearly dragged off by that horrid Georgie Grimsley. He wanted me to go to Gretna Green with him."

"That young rapscallion. He'll not treat my niece so," Uncle said as he pushed past me with a look that bespoke ill for Mr. Grimsley.

I caught his arm. "Don't go, Uncle. The last thing we need is to give the police a reason to pay attention to you."

"Oh. I suppose you're right. But that young pup should not get off scot free after such an insult."

I remembered Georgie holding his eye while rolling around in agony and could not help but chuckle. "He did not get off scot free. I'm afraid he will be sporting a blackened eye for a while thanks to my rather sturdy handbag." I held up the bag to illustrate my point.

Uncle guffawed. "Good show, Petronella. You have a bit of the Percival in you, after all."

"I suppose I get it from both sides of my family. However, I'm afraid I have to report that Georgie Grimsley prevented me from acquiring another Colombian *peso* that was on a seat in the last car. It proves the man in the slouch hat is connected to the other *peso*."

"No matter. We have the other coin."

At that moment James and Jane came down the corridor toward us. "What ho! Did you find anything? We found nothing," said James.

We settled into one of the empty compartments as I explained about Georgie Grimsley and the *peso*. Jane laughed at Georgie's black eye, but James's reaction was much more gratifying. He started up out of his seat, his fists balled up.

"The scoundrel. He'll have more than a black eye when I'm through with him." Could it be that he cared?

Both Jane and I leaped up to stand in his way. "Rather than worry about Georgie Grimsley, we need to develop a battle strategy for when we get to Charing Cross Station," I reasoned.

"Yes," said Jane. "We should be getting there soon." Indeed, the clickety-clack of the train wheels came farther and farther apart.

James sat back down, still muttering, but cooperative enough that by the time we arrived at Charing Cross Station, we had a working plan. I wished that in James's mutters there was something of the lover, but as far as I could tell, he was more worried about the slight to my good name than any danger I might have been in.

Once we disembarked, Jane and I strolled arm in arm through the busy station, making our way from vendor to vendor while Uncle and James departed in different directions to question ticket sellers, guards, and bobbies. At the first stall, I bought newspaper-wrapped fish and chips. "Thank you," I said as the vendor, a plump little woman with cherries hanging from her straw hat, handed me the steaming, fragrant food. "I was supposed to meet my gardener here in the station to choose summer flowers for my estate. You haven't happened to see a man with a dark mustache and slouch hat, have you?" I gave the woman an extra six-pence and a smile.

"Laws, no, dearie. Sorry to say, I ain't seen no one like that. 'Ope you finds 'im, I do."

We proceeded from fish and chips to peppermints to the booksellers to the baker with no more to show for our troubles than several bags of sweets, some sticky buns, and a few newspapers and magazines. We devoured the fish and chips first thing, of course. There's nothing like a properly prepared bit of good old British fish and chips to fortify one, but I would have liked a tidbit or two of information as dessert.

James joined us just in time to enjoy the sticky buns while they were warm. "Where is your uncle, old thing? The bobby over there saw our man heading east."

"The suspect could be going anywhere. How are we going to find him?" asked Jane.

"It is my guess that he is going to find Salas," said James.

There was that name again. "Who is Salas?" Jane and I asked simultaneously.

"If I am correct," said James, "he is Don Hernando Salas, a Colombian aristocrat supposedly exiled in England since their civil war started a few years ago. His estates run into southern Panama, so he would have a lot to lose if Panama declared independence."

"If you know so much about him, where is he?" I asked.

James flashed a smile that smote my heart. The dashed man is too handsome for his own good. "He has a suite at the Savoy."

"Why, that's not far from here," said Jane.

"What is not far from here?" asked Uncle as he approached.

"The Savoy Hotel, Uncle Augustus. Where Don Hernando Salas resides." I noticed that several more bits of paper stuck out from *Insectile Creatures* and that Uncle looked as smug as James. I could only suppose that the insects we had seen on the train had their journeys cut unexpectedly short by Uncle's predations.

"Then shall we go?" Uncle offered me his arm, and we sauntered out of the station and onto the Strand, followed by James and Jane.

The Strand bustled with purposeful people striding this way and that along the sidewalk, while along the street itself flowed horse-drawn hansom and hackney cabs, tradesmen's wagons, the occasional motorcar, and hundreds of bicycles. In fact, the *ching-ching* of bicycle bells drowned out the *clip-clop* of the horses. Occasionally a motorcar sounded its hooter. The bustle was invigorating; however, crossing to the other side of the Strand would have been suicidal. Luckily we were on the same side of the street as the Savoy.

The cacophony of London traffic was such that it took a few seconds for me to register that someone was bellowing behind us. The wild *ching-chinging* of a bicycle warned me to jump to my left. I nearly knocked Uncle off his feet. We both recovered our equilibrium just in time to have a bobby's hat thrust into my arms by the cyclist. I caught a glimpse of his face. Georgie Grimsley! His black eye only served to accentuate his malevolent smirk. He then disappeared into the crowd of bicycles in the street.

"'Ere, 'ere! Young lady, I'll 'ave you know that stealing bobbys' hats is illegal." A red-faced, hatless bobby planted himself in front of us, panting as he rested his hands on his knees.

The hat burned in my grip. I thrust it at the bobby. "I am not accustomed to stealing hats from officers of the law. This hat was thrown at me by a passing cyclist."

"Likely story. Probably a well-planned snatch. Young people of your set 'ave been taking great delight in just such larks of late. I'll wager you know the thief. Wot's 'is name?"

"I do know him, unfortunately, although I am most assuredly not in league with him. His name is Georgie Grimsley." I drew myself up to my full height and attempted to mimic Great-aunt Theophilia, but was woefully short of her aplomb and lacked her lorgnette. I really would have to purchase one soon.

The bobby stuffed his hat onto his head. "Well, I won't 'ave it—this larkin' about by rich young fings taking no account of the law. I'm going to make an example of you. Come along now to the station."

I gawked.

Uncle stepped forward and bowed slightly. "My dear sir. This young lady is my niece and—"

"Then you should be taking better care not to let her get into scrapes." The bobby thrust his jaw out as he glared at Uncle Augustus, who appeared quite speechless at the officer's pugnacity.

I became aware that a large crowd had gathered around us.

"For shame. Wealth brings privilege is what she thinks," said one woman, shielding her little girl with her skirt from my wickedness. Others in the crowd muttered agreement so vehemently that they sounded in danger of turning into a mob.

"Excuse me. Lord James Sinclair here. I saw it all, and the young lady was a victim of the depravity of the perpetrator. She had nothing to do with the theft," James said as he and Jane pushed their way through the throng to stand by my side. James withdrew a card from his wallet and presented it to the bobby.

The bobby studied the card. "All right, sir. 'Ome Office,

is it? Oi suppose Oi must believe you. Oi'm Officer Dudworth." There were exclamations of surprise from the crowd at the revelation that James was connected with the Home Office.

James indicated Uncle and me and his sister. "Officer Dudworth, would you be so good as to escort us to Scotland Yard? We are on our way to speak to Inspector Higginbotham on a matter of some urgency." He glanced at me and I nodded agreement.

"Well, if you're going to Scotland Yard, you're 'eading in the wrong direction. It's that way." He pointed his nightstick in the opposite direction down the Strand from where we'd been going.

James tipped his hat to the officer. "Thank you for setting us to rights, Officer Dudworth. We just emerged from Charing Cross Station, and I'm afraid I got my senses mixed up."

Jane smiled up at the bobby. "You will help us find the Yard, won't you? If our nation's future rested on my brother's sense of direction, we'd all be in the soup."

Chuckles rumbled through the crowd at Jane's comment.

One man called, "Good fing we got coppers to set fings straight, then, ain't it."

Another said, "Aw, take 'em to the Yard. It ain't every day one of them swells admits 'e needs 'elp from a copper."

Officer Dudworth stuck out his chest proudly at the comments. He swaggered as he swung his nightstick in front of him and strode ahead of us. "Clear the way. Oi've got more important fings to do than be a rubbishy tourist guide all day."

We walked willingly in his wake like ducklings following a mother duck, although Uncle harrumphed a bit. I could tell that his dignity was wounded.

"Thank you for rescuing me," I whispered to James and Jane.

"My pleasure," said James. His voice was warm. For a moment I reveled in the illusion that he cared for me as more than a connection of his sister's, before he commented, "Can't have my sister's bosom friend arrested." Oh, well. My hopes had been dashed before, but they would rise again.

"I'm almost sorry you weren't arrested. I've never visited anyone in prison before," Jane whispered, and then burst out laughing at my indignant expression.

Chapter Fourteen

In Which the Horde Hinders

BEING MARCHED THROUGH THE STREETS of London for several blocks by an officious bobby may not be good for one's dignity, but it does have the effect of allowing one to marshal one's thoughts. Upon further contemplation, I decided it was probably for the best that we had been circumvented in our attempts to confront Don Salas. What would we have said or done in the middle of the Savoy? I could not see us inviting him to tea in order to demand the return of the dame and the generalissimo. Should we have revealed our suspicions of espionage over cucumber sandwiches or requested information about his plans for retribution while partaking of petits fours? I think not. On the other hand, it was our duty to show the tiara and *peso* to Inspector Higginbotham —

probably sooner than later. Hopefully, he would listen to us this time.

Once we were inside the entrance of the New Scotland Yard, the bobby's bellicosity deflated somewhat, since he was confronted with an equally officious representative of that venerable institution, who demanded, "And just what do you think you're doing here, Officer?"

Officer Dudworth puffed himself up long enough to say, "Oi'm deliverin' these 'ere culprits to Inspector 'Igginbotham."

James stepped forward and presented his card to the Yard officer. "Please be good enough to let Inspector Higginbotham know that Lord Sinclair is here with additional information."

"Yes, sir." The representative of the Yard sent James's card with a boy who had been sitting nearby, nearly asleep on a chair.

While we waited, the bobby stared at us watchfully, as if we were about to make a break for the doors. He seemed quite disappointed when the messenger returned and reported with great disinterest, "The inspector said to wait 'ere and 'e would be available shortly." Then the boy plunked down in his chair and promptly fell asleep.

James reached to shake the bobby's hand. "Thank you so

much, Officer Dudworth, for delivering us safely. I hope we have not kept you too long from your duties."

The bobby harrumphed a bit, but looked only too happy to leave, now that we'd proven to be respectable.

We sat upon the hard wooden chairs reserved for visitors. As I arranged the flounces of my skirt attractively — and might I add, daringly — about my ankles, I commented, "Well, James. I'm seeing you in a new light. Somehow I'm having a spot of trouble reconciling the image of you as a diplomat with memories of the boy who hung the ostler's trousers on the weathervane or the time you switched the salt for the sugar in your cook's larder."

"Or the time, not two years ago, when he wrote messages on the eggs and put them back under the hens. The kitchen maid nearly had hysterics when she read that the world would end the next day." Jane giggled.

Uncle chimed in, "James, this is a side of you I had not suspected."

James faced forward, a blush infusing even the tips of his ears. "Yes, well, it is a side of me that is in the past."

Jane slid her arm into his and rested her cheek against his shoulder. "Don't be cross, brother dear. It's just that I had not seen you in an official capacity before. I'm really rather impressed."

I held out a bag of sweets to him. "Here. These might help."

"Help what?" said James as he took a few peppermints.

"Cheer you up."

"*Sweeten* me up, don't you mean? The two of you are dashed lucky that I'm such a gentleman, or I might mention a few of your escapades, such as how the ducks got into the wash tubs in the laundry not less than a year ago."

Jane placed a gloved hand over her brother's mouth. "Stop! You're not supposed to know about that one. You were away on holiday."

I stifled a yawn. "I do hope the inspector does not keep us waiting too long, or we shall have aired all our dirty laundry, and Uncle Augustus will have an entirely different view of us. Although I'll wager that Uncle was not above a little clandestine mischief in his time. Am I right, Uncle?"

"A man my age should not have to answer questions about youthful follies," said Uncle Augustus. "Read your newspapers, children, and I shall peruse my book." He tapped *Insectile Creatures*.

We obediently divided up our various newspapers and magazines and set to reading. I was anxious to see if the papers contained anything else about the kidnappings, but they had nothing more than what we knew already. Every few minutes, I glanced at my watch. I sighed. I read some

96

more. I checked my watch against a clock on one wall and adjusted my watch by two minutes. I read some more. Did the inspector mean to make us wait so long? Did he not care that we had information, or did he think we would not have anything of importance? I began to run out of patience, and when I shook the sweets bag, I found I was also out of peppermints.

"Lord Sinclair and party. The inspector is ready to see you now," called the man at the front desk.

After going up some stairs and down a hall, we found Inspector Higginbotham's office. He sat behind a business-like desk, but there were no chairs for us to sit on, which I am quite sure was a conscious effort on his part to make him seem kingly while visitors played the peasants.

Inspector Higginbotham came directly to the point. "Yes? Your message, Lord Sinclair, said that you had more information."

James motioned for me to come forward. "Thank you for seeing us, Inspector. We followed your example after you left and looked for more clues and discovered these not far from where you found the ruby. We thought you should have them."

I drew the tiara and *peso* from my handbag and placed them on the inspector's desk. "Dame Carruthers was wearing that tiara when she was abducted."

"And the coin is from Colombia," Jane chimed in.

The inspector picked up both items and turned them over several times, his mouth pursed in thought. Finally, he said, "These do establish that the dame and generalissimo were there, and the state of the tiara indicates a struggle." He heaved a sigh. "They do not, however, establish who the kidnappers are."

"Petronella! Augustus!" My aunts' voices rang down the hall.

We all stared at one another in horror. Aunts are devastating enough in one's home, but to have them invade Scotland Yard is a desperate situation indeed. Inspector Higginbotham put his forehead on his desk for a moment, as if attempting to draw fortitude from within. So it was that when Great-aunt Theophilia and Aunt Cordelia pushed their way into his office, followed by Cyril, Crimea, and Boeotia, the inspector was able to stand and greet them with more dignity than I thought possible under the circumstances.

"Aha!" Great-aunt Theophilia said upon seeing us. "We thought we'd find you here. Augustus, you simply must not allow Petronella to gallivant among the lower classes in this manner. It is most unseemly."

Boeotia, safe behind her mother's skirts, stuck her tongue out at me, while Crimea looked especially satisfied with my plight.

The inspector strode from behind his desk to shake both aunts' hands. "Why, Lady Worffingdon and Lady Farworthy, how delightful to see you again so soon. I'm sorry I'm not able to offer you seating accommodations, but as you can see, we're rather cramped at the moment." He waved a hand at our group and then at the additional relations.

Aunt Cordelia sniffed. "You should see the taxis in Burma."

I counted ten people in the smallish office. Not bad, but not a record, either. I'd read in the *Times* that some Oxford students had stuffed twenty-eight of themselves into one of the red telephone boxes that had begun to appear on the streets of London.

Great-aunt Theophilia raised her lorgnette and gazed at the inspector as if to cow him. Indeed, he seemed to shrink a little. "Inspector Higginbotham, I demand to know what you are doing with my niece."

The inspector looked astonished. He spluttered, "I'm doing nothing with your niece, Lady Worffingdon. She came here of her own accord."

"And just what do you intend to do about Petronella delivering the ransom? That is not a proper activity for a young girl of good family," said Aunt Cordelia, her monocle screwed firmly in place.

99

Both aunts glared at the inspector, who held up his hands in surrender as he retreated behind his desk.

A voice came from the doorway, which was completely blocked by my beloved relatives. "If that's you there in your office, Inspector 'Igginbotham, you're to go to Mr. Berwick's office immediately."

Inspector Higginbotham rolled his eyes heavenward as if in supplication. "Please excuse me." He squeezed himself as best he could between us and out the door, emerging into the hall rather like a bar of soap that squirts from between two wet hands.

He was gone only a minute or two before the previously heard voice announced from the doorway, "If there's a Miss Arbuthnot in there, her presence is requested in Mr. Berwick's office."

"I'm here." I wriggled through my relations and made it out nearly unscathed, except that Crimea deliberately tripped me so that I fell against James, who caught me to his magnificently broad chest before setting me upright once more. I almost thanked her.

My arms still tingling from the contact with James's hands, I presented myself in Mr. Berwick's office. Thank goodness it had several chairs, because I suddenly found myself rather tired and wishing for a cup of tea. Not surprising, considering what had taken place over the last twenty-four hours. Mr. Berwick waved me toward the seat next to the one Inspector Higginbotham occupied, and I sat.

"So you are the young lady at whose coming-out party Dame Carruthers and Generalissimo Reyes-Cardoza were abducted." Mr. Berwick sounded hearty and grandfatherly, in the manner a man of his age might speak to a deaf three-year-old. He even smiled at me in a grandfatherly way.

"Yes, sir." I was bewildered by his tone.

Mr. Berwick held up the ransom note that had been delivered to my house. "You are also mentioned on this note." He beamed at me. What was he getting at?

"Yes, sir. It is addressed to me." I was trying not to be annoyed at being treated like a child.

The odious man waggled his finger at me, still beaming. "That's not all. You are also instructed to be the one to deliver the ransom money to the base of Lord Nelson's Column."

I bit the inside of my cheek to keep from saying something I would regret. I managed to smile back at Mr. Berwick through clenched teeth. "Yes, sir."

"Well, this won't do. It won't do at all."

I blinked. "What won't do?"

Inspector Higginbotham cleared his throat. "What Mr. Berwick is saying is that not only would it be dangerous for

101

you to be the one to deliver the ransom, it could cause repercussions internationally if you botched it."

I blinked again. Botched it? Astonishing. Taking a deep breath, I said, "Do you have some idea that I *want* to deliver the ransom?"

"Well, you are a sixteen-year-old girl. Life must seem a romantic romp at your age," said Mr. Berwick. He smiled sympathetically. I was taking a dislike to his smiles.

"I can assure you that I have no intention of delivering the ransom," I said. Indeed, I could think of nothing I would like to do less than be a puppet whose strings were being pulled on the one side by Scotland Yard and on the other by kidnappers.

Now it was the turn of Mr. Berwick and Inspector Higginbotham to blink in surprise. Mr. Berwick exclaimed, "But you must. There is no one else to do it. They will be watching for you in particular."

"Then why did you say it wouldn't do and repercussions and all that?"

"We were only alluding to the possibilities of danger to convince you of the seriousness of the situation, and then we were going to explain our contingency plans," said Mr. Berwick, obviously resenting the way I was not following the prescribed script.

At that moment the horde pushed their way into Mr. Berwick's office. Great-aunt Theophilia demanded, "*Now* what are you doing with our niece?"

Inspector Higginbotham shrank back in his chair. Mr. Berwick, however, stood. Towering over my aunt, he said, "My good lady, whoever you are, we are trying to convince your niece to do her duty in a matter of importance to Mother England."

The aunts looked taken aback, and my estimation of Mr. Berwick rose.

"Well," said Great-aunt Theophilia.

"Just what exactly do you intend our niece to do? You have not even asked for our permission," said Aunt Cordelia, her chin jutting in such a pugnacious manner that she reminded me of Officer Dudworth.

Uncle Augustus stepped between my aunts and Mr. Berwick. "If there is any permission to be asked, it will be of me. I am Petronella's guardian, after all."

Aunts and Uncle glared at one another. Cyril gave a rather hysterical giggle. However, it was Crimea grinning at me as if immensely pleased with my dilemma that decided me.

"Ahem," I said, and all eyes swiveled in my direction. "I believe the decision ultimately rests with me. I have decided to deliver the ransom."

Chapter Fifteen

In Which More Than One Is All Wet

WHEN ONE HAS BEEN RASH enough to commit oneself to performing a risky task in the service of one's country, quite outside of one's experience, one is at the mercy of all kinds of irrational thoughts while waiting to perform said task. For instance, I thought of my relations' violent disapproval of my decision, the protests of James and Jane, that Uncle Augustus tucked into *Insectile Creatures* a centipede he found in the corner of Mr. Berwick's office, and that the cloak supplied to me by the Yard to ward off the chill of the night was at least ten years out of fashion. Fortunately, not many people would see me wearing it, since I was to deliver the ransom at midnight.

I now stood at the base of the statue of Charles the First across from Lord Nelson's Column on Trafalgar Square as the pea soup that is London fog swirled about me. Through the thick mist I could faintly see glowing circles of light; they were the street lamps surrounding the square. My hands felt cold even through my gloves, mostly from apprehension.

Although I couldn't see it, I knew that near the closest edge of that square, across from where I stood, reared the tallest Corinthian column in the world, of which we English are justly proud, and on top of that column stood the statue of Lord Nelson — he who had saved Britain from Napoleon at the Battle of Trafalgar. I hoped he could, figuratively speaking, help save us again — this time from another enemy trying to destroy Mother England.

Mist-muffled footsteps sounded next to me, and my heart shuddered in alarm.

"Hello, old egg," said James from near my ear.

"What are you doing here?" I whispered, my heart fluttering both from the unexpectedness of his presence and his presence. Through my cloak, I could feel the warmth of his arm against mine.

"Scouting about a bit. Did you know your aunt, the Duchess of Worffingdon, and her two offspring are armed with walking sticks over by the plinth supporting King George's statue?"

I groaned.

"Oh, it doesn't stop there. Your aunt Cordelia is bravely

holding down Sir Charles Napier's plinth on the opposite corner, only she has an umbrella. She says the end is quite sharp."

"And Cyril?" I asked.

"Cyril is cowering next to the base of the empty fourth plinth. I don't think he likes fog. He keeps sniveling."

"What about the inspector?"

"Inspector Higginbotham and Sergeant Crumple keep slinking from plinth base to plinth base trying to convince your relations to leave or at least hush. You can imagine their lack of success. There is no sign, however, of your uncle." James sounded a trifle worried over the last bit.

I was worried too. "Not knowing where he is does little to calm me, and neither does knowing where my other relations are. I might have guessed they would try something like this. I am surprised you found anyone in this pea soup. However, you haven't mentioned Jane."

"I've ensconced her safely in the Savoy with a late supper. She is supposed to be holding a table for you and me to which we can retire once this muddle is quite finished."

"However did you convince her to stay away from such an adventure?"

James chuckled, although his voice hinted at grimness. "She insisted. When I checked in at the Home Office, I was told that Don Hernando Salas is supposedly meeting an accomplice from the Colombian embassy at the Savoy Grill tonight. Jane's determined to overhear their plans. I only allowed her to stay because she should be safe enough surrounded by other diners."

"At least she'll have dinner," I said disconsolately, thinking of the weak tea that had been my repast at the Yard, where I had spent the evening while being briefed on my role in delivering the ransom money. "I only hope I can find my way in this fog to Nelson's Column at the appropriate time."

"I wish you could be persuaded to join Jane."

I wished I were with Jane as well, but I would not like James to know. He would think me a wet goose. I was damp and shivering from the cold, but I was not a goose. "The note specifically stated it was I who should deliver the money." I pushed against the satchel at my feet with my toe, feeling its solidity, a firmness made possible by several bundles of good English pounds. "Oh, where is Uncle? It's impossible to properly worry about oneself when one's dearest relation is running amok in London. There can't be many insects for him to find in this weather."

"It's a pity we lost him. He'll turn up," said James. I didn't know whether to be comforted or to laugh insanely at the number of odd situations where Uncle might turn up.

Big Ben began to bong midnight, sounding ghostly and far away.

"It's time." I picked up the satchel and nearly toppled over under its weight. "Off to the column and the depiction of Lord Nelson's death. Rather fitting, isn't it?"

"I'll come with you," said James.

"No. The note said only I was to come."

"They'll never see me in the fog."

The thought of James keeping close steadied me immeasurably. "Wait a few seconds and follow me, then, but stay far enough away so they don't see you."

Under the weight of the satchel, I staggered like a drunken man across the road and to the column, past the statues of lions at its base. I deposited the satchel just under the plaque depicting Lord Nelson's sagging body supported by his friends. My heart pounded from the effort and fear. I did not like being unable to see what was around me. If only I could see who was coming, I might not have been so afraid. I heard a creak as if a door opened and I waited, puzzled. Where was a door in Trafalgar Square close enough to hear it creak?

A stirring of air brushed my cheek as if someone had moved quite close by. I spun about, breathless. Something brushed my other cheek. I whirled in that direction.

"Where are you? I brought the money." I sounded quite faint, not at all like the heroine I imagined myself to be.

A low voice with a foreign accent said near my ear, "Give me the money."

"Where are the dame and the generalissimo?" There. I sounded much more firm. I stepped back a little from the satchel.

A breathy chuckle. "Come back tomorrow night at the same time. I will count the money, and if it is all there, I'll leave the directions here at the base of the column."

The fog swirled as if someone had left.

"Wait!" I called, only to hear a whooshing noise as if someone had leaped a great distance. There was a thud. A shout. Uncle Augustus? Then a tremendous splash and another shout. Great-aunt Theophilia? Then several splashes and much more shouting. Aunt Cordelia? Crimea? Boeotia? Cyril? No, not Cyril. Inspector Higginbotham? Sergeant Crumple? It seemed that James and I were the only ones still dry.

Chapter Sixteen

In Which a Friend Goes Missing

WHEN ONE OBSERVES ONE'S ESTEEMED relations, as well as representatives of Scotland Yard, standing dripping wet in the grand foyer of the Savoy at one o'clock in the morning, one has cause to reflect that the power to intimidate is somehow lost when the intimidators are soaking wet and shivering pitifully. It seems that in the thick fog, various aunts and cousins and Yard detectives had forgotten entirely about the fountains that had been placed strategically in Trafalgar Square in order to discourage rioting. I decided that whoever came up with the plan to build fountains in the name of crowd control obviously understood what I was just observing—that wet and shivering people lose threat value.

After listening to all the garbled accounts, it became clear to me that Uncle Augustus had leaped from the top of the column onto the kidnapping conspirator and bowled him into aunts and cousins and detectives, knocking the lot in a domino effect into one of the fountains. Unfortunately, in the melee that followed, the kidnapper had escaped. However, he left the rather soggy, still-full satchel amid the pennies that tourists on holiday had thrown into the fountains.

My attention was brought back to the Savoy Hotel's front hall by my cousin Crimea crying, "Mummy, just look at my new frock. And I was going to wear it to Jessalyn St. John's garden party. I don't care if England has problems with international transport. I'm not ruining any more frocks."

Boeotia's wailing drowned out her older sister's protestations. "I don't like playing tenpins, let alone *being* a tenpin."

Aunt Cordelia glared at the two girls as if they were unworthy of being Arbuthnots on their mother's side. I noticed that Uncle Augustus, still carrying *Insectile Creatures* under his arm, was the only one, besides myself and James, who was not dripping on the rich Savoy carpet—a fact that the hand-wringing night concierge also noted. He approached Uncle Augustus.

"Sir, whatever shall we do with all of these . . . these . . ." I could see the wheels of reason turning in his brain, albeit slowly. He was probably thinking that if he protested too vehemently, he might lose customers. However, if he did not take care of the situation immediately, he might lose his other customers. I could hear several in the dining room, most probably celebrating after an evening's entertainment in the theaters of the famed West End. I imagined they might be offended by the sight of so many less than properly attired people inhabiting one of the world's bastions of respectability.

To my surprise, Uncle acted with aplomb, decision, and intelligence. "My good man, if you have a private room where we may retire, as well as several blankets and towels, we may be assured of a solution to this sticky situation, and you will reap the gratitude of several people of consequence as well as receiving appropriate remuneration."

Uncle saw the look of disbelief on the concierge's face and added, "I can promise you that this mélange of seeming miscreants includes a duchess, a lady, a Scotland Yard inspector, and several offspring of the aforementioned aristocracy."

The mention of remuneration tipped the balance in favor of providing the private room, blankets, and towels. The concierge assumed an expression of extreme unctuousness as he proclaimed to the dripping group, "Ladies and gentlemen, if you would follow me, I have a suitable accommodation where you will be properly cared for." As he left the grand front hall, he clapped his hands at a couple of housemaids hovering wide-eyed in a doorway and said, "Towels. Blankets. The private dining room. Immediately."

The maids scurried appropriately. My relations and the Yard personnel followed the concierge dutifully and damply. They left a large dark and dank spot, slightly off center, in the front hall and a trail of wet footprints leading toward the private dining room. I mused that it would take a detective of no great ability to find us, but as my gaze lighted upon Inspector Higginbotham's dripping back, I seriously doubted whether it was a detective of any great ability who had made some of the sodden footprints in the first place. Uncle, James, and I also made our way to the dining room.

The thought of detecting brought to mind several questions left unresolved by our exploits. How did the kidnapper get to Nelson's Column undetected when so many people were searching for him? What was that creaking-door sound I had heard just before the kidnapper appeared at my side? How were we going to find Dame Carruthers and Generalissimo Reyes-Cardoza now? Was their abduction a diversion? What was I to do with all of these drenched people, many of whom were my guests? These and many other questions rattled around in my brain.

Crimea pushed by me, obviously still in a temper over her frock. "Pig's tail," she spat as she passed me. I blanched at the mention of one of the least dignified episodes of my young life and glanced about hoping no one had heard.

As I walked by the concierge, who was holding open the door, I asked, "Would you please bring pots of hot tea and some biscuits and perhaps some sandwiches." I slipped him several pounds and saw that my consequence rose immeasurably in his estimation.

Inspector Higginbotham, now draped with a large woolen blanket, was holding forth nearly nose to nose with the similarly draped Great-aunt Theophilia. "I daresay that if not for your interference, we might have caught the man," he said.

Great-aunt Theophilia, eyes narrowed and lorgnette raised, stared the unfortunate inspector down. "And I daresay, if not for your incompetence, we might have caught the man ourselves, especially since I had got hold of the kidnapper's coat." She held up a piece of dark cloth that looked to be a coat pocket ripped from its original garment. "It did not help in the least to be suddenly sat upon by such a great oaf as yourself midfountain."

At that moment, maids and waiters entered bearing blankets and towels, as well as trays of steaming pots of tea and several plates of biscuits and sandwiches. James—bless his handsome heart—and Uncle immediately took control of the situation by passing around cups of tea and asking whether people wanted milk and one lump of sugar or two lumps. Uncle whisked bits of paper from his book from time to time.

I watched with satisfaction. All of my guests were being taken care of—except Jane.

My hands flew to my mouth as I suddenly remembered my bosom friend, still in the dining room. I raced out the door. As I hurried toward the famous Savoy Grill, I could hear the clink of silver and crystal and the laughter of late-night revelers giddy from the kind of entertainment offered in the West End and the Savoy.

The maître d'hôtel met me at the entrance to the dining room with a disdainful expression. I knew it was unusual for an unescorted female to enter the Grill, especially at this hour. Drawing myself erect and gazing down my nose at the man, I said, "I am joining the party of Miss Sinclair. Please take me to her."

The maître d'hôtel gave a slight bow. "I regret to inform you that Miss Sinclair left some time ago in the company of Don Hernando Salas."

Chapter Seventeen

In Which a Pocket's Contents Are Revealed

HOW DOES ONE TELL ONE'S bosom friend's brother, and the object of one's desire, that said friend has disappeared? Even more important, where *was* Jane? Was she safe? My heart raced faster than I could hasten back to the private dining room.

"James. Jane. Jane. James," I gabbled as I grasped James's arm and drew him away from where he was coaxing Boeotia into eating a biscuit instead of wailing.

"What are you trying to say, old twig?" James patted my hand on his arm in a brotherly fashion. Even in these direst of circumstances I could not stop my traitorous heart from fluttering at his touch.

I forced myself to concentrate on the task at hand. "Jane. She's not in the Savoy Grill."

"Can't that girl follow simple instructions? I shall have to talk to her about gadding about by herself in London. It just isn't done." James frowned.

"She was not alone when she left," I said. "She left the Grill with Don Hernando Salas."

James's face drained of all color. He grasped me by the shoulders as if he would shake me. "Salas! This is terrible. He's a dangerous man."

At that moment, Uncle Augustus approached us, carrying the pocket pinched by Great-aunt Theophilia, as well as his book *Insectile Creatures*. "I think we may have found a clue, or rather, two clues." Great-aunt Theophilia and Aunt Cordelia followed him.

"It was I who pulled the pocket from the scoundrel," Great-aunt Theophilia said proudly.

James and I gaped at Uncle and my aunts. In light of Jane's disappearance, I had forgotten, and I suppose that James had as well, that our original quest had been to find Dame Carruthers and Generalissimo Reyes-Cardoza.

I shook my head to clear it. "Not now, Uncle. Jane has disappeared. She may have been kidnapped, too. She was taken from the Grill by Don Hernando Salas. We must go search for her."

James said, "Wait. Perhaps these clues are doubly important. It is likely that Don Hernando Salas has some connection with the kidnappers of the dame and generalissimo. There can't be too many international kidnappers infesting England at the same time."

Uncle laid the heavy book on a nearby table, extracted three small sheets of waxed paper from it, and spread them out. From the still-damp pocket he withdrew a large beetle like the one he had ingested and two tiny insects that looked like some kind of fly. He laid each insect on its own piece of waxed paper and then leafed through the book.

Uncle's hand hesitated over a bit of waxed paper that contained a particularly fat moth, but he managed to resist. When he came to a page two-thirds of the way through the book and pointed, James and I leaned over to look.

"As you can see, these two smaller insects from the pocket are a type of small fly found only near the piers of the river Thames. Right there in the book." Uncle's finger tapped a drawing of a fly.

James straightened up. "So the man has been at the docks. That means we are looking for a Colombian ship berthed at the docks along the Thames," said James, thereby demonstrating that his shoulders are not the only well-muscled part of his body.

"It must be a cargo ship that has been there for at least several days, which would explain how the foreign-looking logs came to England," I said, not to be outdone.

James stared at me as if I had said something brilliant, which I had. Then he struck his forehead with his right palm. "Of course. Our intelligence said something about Don Hernando Salas having just returned from a long visit to Colombia."

"Then if Jane is with Don Hernando Salas, she may very well be where Dame Carruthers and Generalissimo Reyes-Cardoza are as well," I said.

Across the room Cyril suddenly leaped to his feet shouting, "I will not have cucumber sandwiches thrust down my back." He dashed after Boeotia, who uttered a squeal and dived under one of the tables. Behind the two of them Crimea smiled with satisfaction. Aunt Cordelia marched over to Crimea and brought her umbrella down on her elder niece's head with a *thwunk*.

Great-aunt Theophilia swung around just in time to see Aunt Cordelia's umbrella connect with Crimea's head. Grabbing her walking stick, Great-aunt Theophilia rushed after Aunt Cordelia. Aunt Cordelia faced her with raised umbrella. "No, you don't, Theophilia. I won't have your spoiled chits bothering my Cyril again."

"Compared to your toad of a son, my chits, as you call them, are paragons of virtue," shouted Great-aunt Theophilia, walking stick held forth in accusation.

James took my arm. "We have to go. I must tell the home

secretary what we've learned and get help looking for Jane."

I decided to throw hostessing duties to the winds in favor of national security, friendship, and the opportunity to have James's arm through mine and went with him.

"I think I'll come with you." Uncle hastily followed us, eyeing the feuding aunts with trepidation.

Chapter Eighteen

In Which the Home Secretary Is at Home

AS A YOUNG GIRL, ONE imagines all sorts of marvelous adventures. As for myself, I had imagined a number of episodes that included riding in a carriage in the middle of the night. All of them had been of a romantic nature. A few of them had fog swirling about the horses and past the carriage lamps. Several had included James at my side. The James in my imaginary adventures had held my gloved hands fervently in his and had let sweet compliments fall like ripened plums into my shell-like ears. I imagined leaning toward those firm, well-shaped lips that were speaking the fruity tributes until my own lips nearly touched his. At this point I could imagine no further, having not had the experience of being kissed. But one can always hope.

However, at the moment, James—sitting in the carriage

next to me with the fog swirling past the windows—ignored me as he fumed. Once or twice he punched his fist into his open palm. Sometimes he muttered. I thought I heard him say, "Why was I fool enough to leave her?" At least twice he said, "Where could she be?"

I must admit my thoughts were the same. I am also ashamed to admit that I was just the tiniest bit disappointed that my first experience at night with James in a carriage occured under these circumstances. For one thing, I never thought Uncle Augustus would sit across from us, absently pulling slips of waxed paper from *Insectile Creatures*, extracting the contents, and chewing contemplatively.

Truth to tell, I was too overwrought by Jane's disappearance to care that Uncle Augustus accompanied us. Whatever possessed the girl to leave the safety of the Savoy Grill with Don Hernando Salas? He sounded like one of the characters in those lurid novels by Millicent Pinktowers that my governesses had never let me read, but that I had found under their pillows just the same. I'd never actually cared to read one. But from the large number of books accumulated by various governesses, I knew Miss Pinktowers was a prolific and popular authoress. At the moment, though, I could not have cared less what the characters were named in any of Miss Pinktowers's lurid novels. I just wanted Jane back safe and sound.

Another element of adventure that I had not taken into account was the cold, which caused me considerable discomfort. I should have known that fog, romantic as it might seem, would be damp, dismal, and decidedly nippy. I was certainly aware of it now as I huddled on the hard seat of the carriage, longing for the comfort of my own bedroom and fireplace and wondering if Jane was doing the same. Unfortunately, I could not expect the home secretary to have a warm fire going at this hour of the morning. He and all of his servants were probably snugly in bed, where they ought to be.

Therefore I was surprised when the carriage pulled up in front of a brightly lit building, with purposeful men striding in and out of the front doors.

"I wonder what has happened?" James said as he exited the carriage and helped me down the one step.

"Looks like old Chumpy is in a spot of trouble," said Uncle Augustus, joining James and me on the sidewalk.

"Chumpy?" James and I said together.

"Sir Alastair Dibb, the home secretary. You know him, don't you, James? Working for the man and all?" Uncle pushed at something with the toe of his shoe. I did not want to know what it was. At least he did not pick it up, although he did pat *Insectile Creatures* rather absently.

"Sir Alastair? Of course I know him," sputtered James. "But Chumpy?"

"Naturally. We were at school together. Eton and all that. Then Cambridge. Well, let's see what kind of a faradiddle old Chumpy has got himself into this time. He never was one to stay out of trouble for long. I remember the time he got his nose caught in the headmaster's faucet." Uncle Augustus mounted the stairs to the home secretary's front door, leaving James and me looking at each other incredulously.

James gave a rather doubtful chuckle. "Sir Alastair's nose in a faucet. Unbelievable." He also went up the front steps, and I followed.

There was no need to knock on the door, since it was opened wide, thereby ruining any hope I had of getting warm in a cozy parlor. When James and I entered, Uncle was already in conversation with a harassed-looking gentleman amid the bustle of several serious men who were likely government officials.

Uncle saw us and said, "James, there you are. Come here and let Chumpy tell you what has happened. Petronella, you come along as well."

As James and I approached the home secretary, I could not help but notice that his nose was rather long and pointy. Try as I might to concentrate on what he had to tell us, my attention kept wandering back to his nose. I blinked and tried harder to focus on what the man was telling us.

Sir Alastair was saying, "And there it was — King Edward hung in effigy on the gates of Buckingham Palace. Most distressing. It was a rather good likeness, though, if I do say so myself."

"How dreadful," I said.

"Too true, dear. It's likely to kick up a bit of a dust in the newspapers. Pity. We're having enough trouble keeping the lid on things over the disappearance of Dame Carruthers and Generalissimo Reyes-Cardoza," said Sir Alastair.

"That's why we're here, Sir Alastair," said James. "We think we have a clue." James indicated to the home secretary to follow him into the parlor, where indeed there was a cozy fire. We settled around a small table near the fireplace, and I sighed with relief at the warmth that began to spread through me.

"Look what was found this evening in the coat pocket belonging to one of the kidnappers." James motioned to Uncle, who drew his folded handkerchief from his own pocket and laid it out on the table to display the flies.

Before he could explain what they were, Uncle Augustus said, "Show them what was attached to the effigy, Chumpy."

Sir Alastair drew a piece of note paper from his pocket and laid it next to the beetle and flies on Uncle's handkerchief. All of us craned forward. James and I gasped. On what looked like much the same type of paper as the notes we had received were written the words "Death to the aristocracy." The words were horrible enough. But what made us gasp was the Tou-eh-mah-mah butterfly affixed to the note.

Chapter Nineteen

In Which a Telephone Proves Its Worth

ALTHOUGH UNCLE AUGUSTUS WAS MY dearest relative, I could not help but be a trifle annoyed with him. I was quickly learning that when one's loved one has an alternative source of nourishment, he often forgets to be concerned with one's sustenance in spite of his affection for one. In other words, compulsions take precedence over relations.

I was famished. I had eaten nothing since tea nearly eight hours earlier. Uncle, on the other hand, kept starvation at bay by sneaking snacks from between the pages of his book and stealthily ridding the home secretary's parlor of two or three spiders found in the near proximity of the fireplace, as well as several dead flies from the windowsills. At first, I was alarmed that someone might notice his predations, but his hands moved so rapidly that even I, who knew what he was perpetrating, saw only a blur. I did rap his knuckles, though, when I caught a motion out of the corner of my eye and one of the London dock flies disappeared from James's hand-kerchief, which was still spread out on the table.

"Ouch!" cried Uncle, holding his knuckles. He frowned at me.

I frowned back at him, looked pointedly at the remaining insects, and shook my head in warning.

"It was only one and there's still another," Uncle hissed at me so the others could not hear. "The flies from the sills are so dried out they're hardly satisfying. I just wanted to see if the sea air gave those dock flies any more flavor."

"But they're clues. How are we going to find Jane and the dame and generalissimo if you eat all the clues?" I hissed back.

He pouted. "But you already know what they are and where they come from. It can't hurt to have tried just one."

He sounded so wounded that I relented. "Look, dear Un-cle, over there by the curio cabinet. Some moths have come in the front door and are flying about the gaslight."

Uncle's face lit up immediately. Humming what he prob-ably thought was an innocent tune, but which I recognized as one sung by Weems the underbutler when he'd come back from the local tavern near dawn one morning, Uncle sidled over to the curio cabinet and leaned against it nonchalantly.

When I looked in his direction again, the moths were gone. At least *his* hunger was being satisfied.

Mine, on the other hand, was not. My stomach rumbled in alarming fashion. If I had been less of an Arbuthnot or a Percival, I probably would have felt faint as well.

James also thought nothing of food because he had no need to. He had imbibed two or three cups of hot, sweet tea and devoured several sandwiches and biscuits at the Savoy while I had been inquiring after Jane. At the moment, however, he was using one of those contraptions invented by Mr. Alexander Graham Bell to contact the dock master. Lying open before him was a set of London dock charts with numbered berths.

The home secretary stood nearby, beaming proudly at the way his telephone was being put to good use. "Harrumph. What a modern miracle. When they diddled over the cost of its installation in my residence, I told Parliament that it should come in handy someday. How I shall laugh in Lord Bertram's face."

James held his hand up and waved it at us. "Hush! I can't hear."

Sir Alastair seemed suitably chastised as he crept over to my side. He whispered in my ear, "The only problem is that you have to have someone on the other end who also has one of those contraptions, or they're no use

129

at all. Inconvenient, what? I can hardly think they will catch on."

"Yes," said James. "Ships that came from Colombia or elsewhere in South or Central America docked within the last fortnight. Yes, yes. I know Colombia is in South America. That is why I said *elsewhere*." He rolled his eyes in our general direction as if to say he was speaking to an idiot. My heart fluttered. Even while rolling his eyes, James was still a feast for mine.

James listened for several seconds to the tinny voice coming from the earpiece of the telephone. The voice seemed excessively agitated. James continued in a much more conciliatory tone. "Yes, sir. I understand that it is difficult to think properly at this hour of the morning." He listened again. "What's that you say? There are five ships at the docks that have recently come from that area?"

The tinny voice grew louder.

James wrote furiously on a piece of paper thrust under his pencil by the home secretary. "Yes, I have a pencil. And which ones have specifically come from Colombia? Two? The *Star* and the *Constanza*? At the Royal Albert Dock? Thank you very much. Please do go back to bed, and may you enjoy what is left of the night." He gently placed the earpiece back into its cradle on the telephone.

I was excited. "The *Star* or the *Constanza*. They must be

on one of those two ships. Now we only have to find a way to get them off." My excitement died as I considered possibilities. "Oh, dear. I don't suppose we can simply barge in with hundreds of government personnel and take them back. They could be killed."

James turned to the home secretary. "Sir Alastair, how many men could you muster in the next hour? I have the beginnings of a plan, and by the time the men are here, I shall have it completed."

Uncle Augustus wandered over to our little group. "Chumpy, old friend. I'm sure that James's plan is quite brilliant, but while you are rounding up your contingent, I think I'll wander down to the docks for a bit of a reconnaissance mission. By the time you and your men come, I may be able to offer some additional information."

At that moment, Sir Alastair's butler entered, followed by two footmen, all of whom were bearing trays with tea and several plates of sandwiches. My stomach rumbled audibly at the sight of so much food. However, I could not help but stare at Uncle suspiciously. What kind of reconnaissance did he intend to conduct down on the docks? I should never let him go there by himself. I glanced longingly at the tea and sandwiches and then back at Uncle, who had a look that seemed to say he was hiding his true intentions. Knowing Uncle as I did, I would be a fool to let him go. But I was so hungry. Food or Uncle? Food or Jane? Food or Mother England?

I sighed deeply. "Uncle, I am going with you." My stomach rumbled, but I ignored it. I am an Arbuthnot, after all — and the Percivals are no slouches, either.

"Dear girl," protested Sir Alastair. "That would be most unseemly. Young ladies simply don't . . . don't . . . gallivant."

I began to see why he was called Chumpy and wondered if he was acquainted with my aunts. However, I smiled sweetly. "And what could be more decorous than a young lady's guardian, er . . . guarding her on her way home after an evening's gaiety? Uncle Augustus would look much less suspicious walking along the docks with me on his arm. We could pretend he is giving me a tour or a lecture on the benefits of foreign travel for one's education."

James guffawed. "At four o'clock in the morning? Young ladies don't stroll about the Royal Albert Dock at four o'clock in the morning, even with their guardians." Although James's laughter irritated me, he looked absolutely endearing, with a dark shadow of beard just beginning to appear. I longed to stroke his cheek to feel its roughness even as I longed to punch him in the jaw for being so obstructive and medieval. This was no longer the 1500s, when King Henry could lock up his female acquaintances at will and chop off their heads whenever he pleased. This was a new century —

the 1900s—when females could be the equal of any male—a sentiment I heartily agreed with.

Uncle surprised me by saying, "It would most likely be for the best if Petronella did accompany me. Two pairs of eyes are better than one. It is just getting light, and soon the sailors and dockworkers will be up and about, and I should welcome Petronella's help. Come, dear."

"Coming, Uncle." I grabbed a handful of sandwiches in a most unladylike manner, determined to eat them in the carriage on the way to the docks. Then I followed my uncle out the door of the parlor only to be halted in midstride by the sight of my own esteemed butler, Moriarty.

I blinked and blinked again, afraid that my hunger and lack of sleep were giving me hallucinations. What was my butler doing in London? Moreover, what was my elegant butler doing in London looking as though he had been dragged through a hedgerow backward and breathing heavily as if he had just completed a marathon?

Moriarty bowed exquisitely and presented a small white envelope. "For you, Miss Arbuthnot."

Then he fainted.

I immediately knelt by Moriarty's side, reached into the pocket of his coat, and withdrew the Vile Vial. Swiftly unstopping the small cobalt blue bottle, I waved it under Moriarty's nose. His entire body went rigid. His eyes flew open.

133

He leaped to his feet gasping and clasping his throat with both hands while he staggered about the room.

I smiled with secret satisfaction. Just deserts. I popped the cork back in the bottle with a slap of the palm and handed him back his smelling salts. "There you go, Moriarty. Your salts did the trick . . . as always." My butler was still choking and unable to reply, but I could tell he got my meaning quite well.

James held up the envelope that Moriarty had delivered. On the outside of the envelope was affixed a small butterfly.

Uncle Augustus peered over my shoulder as we all stared. Then Uncle and James and I said together, "But that is *not* a Tou-eh-mah-mah butterfly."

Chapter Twenty

In Which the Butler Is Accused

TO HAVE ONE'S BUTLER APPEAR suddenly at the home secretary's residence at four o'clock in the morning was unsettling, but not so unsettling that one could not eat. I took a bite of sandwich while Uncle opened the note. "Why, it's addressed to Petronella, and it says that if she does not wrap five thousand pounds in brown paper and deliver it to the base of Big Ben by noon, the generalissimo and the dame will be blown to smithereens."

"*Smithereens?* Hardly sounds like a word a Colombian would use," said James.

I took another bite and chewed while I ruminated on the contents of the note. Five thousand pounds is quite a bit of money, even for me. Still, the amount seemed odd. There had been twenty thousand pounds in the satchel, as was demanded in the first ransom note. Why did they now ask for only five thousand? I took another bite of sandwich and noticed for the first time that it was roast beef with a bit of pickle. Happily, I like roast beef. Unhappily, I detest pickles. I ate it anyway.

James took the note from Uncle and carried it over to the table where the note from the effigy rested. "Look. The handwriting is completely different, and so is the paper."

Uncle, thumbing through his *Insectile Creatures*, halted on a page and pointed with his index finger at an illustration that did indeed look like the butterfly on the envelope. "See here. That butterfly on the note has no connection whatsoever with Colombia or Panama. It is a common Wood White, or *Leptidea sinapis*, most often found in English and Welsh woodlands."

"Upon my word, these kidnappers are becoming bilingual as far as butterflies go," said Sir Alastair.

"Not bilingual, by George," said James. "This note was not written by the kidnappers."

I considered James's statement. "Moriarty. How did you come by this note, and however did you find us?" I asked before starting in on a chicken sandwich.

Moriarty, still recovering from the effects of the Vile Vial, looked up from where he had been sitting on the sofa with his head in his hands. "It was tacked to the front door. Someone pulled on the bell, and when I answered I found it."

The attention of everyone in the room riveted on my butler.

"And at what time did you find the note?" I asked.

"It was at eleven-thirty, Miss Arbuthnot, when the bell rang. I had just wound the clock in the front hall as is my custom every evening at eleven-thirty." Moriarty tugged his clothing into place as he rose from the sofa, evidently feeling more like his butlering self by the minute.

"There you are!" said James. "Then it absolutely could not have been the kidnapper who placed the note on the door at your home in the country. There would scarcely have been time for the kidnapper to get back to meet you at Lord Nelson's Column at midnight. The only train at that time of night arrives from London at 10:30 and returns at 11:43."

As James spoke, I could not help but notice that he looked absolutely stunning with disheveled hair. My longing to punch him had long since passed. Now I desired only to smooth his locks into place.

"There are several Wood Whites in the woods on your grounds, Petronella," said Uncle Augustus, absently patting his insect book. I wondered how many of my Wood Whites were squashed between slips of waxed paper in those pages.

Uncle continued, "Whoever wrote the note most likely acquired the butterfly in the vicinity of your home."

"But the only people left at my home are my servants," I said.

All eyes, which had been on Moriarty, then James, then Uncle, now swiveled back toward Moriarty.

"Seize the butler!" shouted Sir Alastair. "I should have known. It is always the butler who does it, whatever it is. Seize him, I say."

"No!" I cried.

Dashing in from the front hall, two government men, indistinguishable from all the other government men we had seen, grabbed Moriarty's arms from behind. "We have him, sir."

Sir Alastair shook his fist in my butler's face. "Where are they? Where have you hidden the dame, the generalissimo, and Miss Sinclair, you fiend?"

Moriarty looked absolutely stunned. "I have no idea what you are talking about . . . sir."

"Of course he doesn't!" I protested.

The home secretary ignored me. "Trying to play innocent, is he? He is obviously in league with the kidnappers. He and only he knew of the plans for the party and was there when the first notes arrived, as well as this latest note. Take him away and lock him up."

"But I have no idea where those people are. And what of Miss Sinclair? Where is she?" Moriarty began struggling. "I've known her since she was a child. If anyone has harmed her . . ." He nearly broke free, but the government men grasped him even more tightly.

"But what of the different handwriting on the notes? Moriarty obviously did not write all of the notes. And what of the different butterflies?" protested James.

"Quite right," I agreed, but no one paid the least attention to me. I was beginning to feel invisible.

"He's in league with the kidnappers. They took turns writing the notes, and I suppose they ran out of Colombian butterflies," said Sir Alastair obdurately. "Take him away to prison."

"Miss Arbuthnot!" wailed Moriarty as the government men hustled him toward the door.

"Wait! He has not said how he came to find us here," I said. "No one knew we were coming here. You cannot take him away until we find out." That got their attention.

The government men ceased their hustling. They seemed to be as curious to know as the rest of us.

"Well, man?" asked Sir Alastair.

Moriarty assumed an air of injured dignity. "I came on the train as fast as I could after I found the note and went straight to the Sinclairs' London residence, where I assumed

139

Miss Arbuthnot would be staying with Miss Sinclair. It seems that Lord Sinclair here had telephoned his man to tell him that he would not be in tonight because of business at the home secretary's residence. I had to run most of the way because there were no cabs to be had at this time of the morning."

Now we all looked at James.

He shrugged. "True. I did phone after I talked to the dock master."

"That information still does not clear the butler of wrong-doing," persisted Sir Alastair.

"Chumpy, old egg. You cannot be serious about imprisoning Miss Arbuthnot's butler. There is not enough evidence," said Uncle.

"And I protest," I said. "I vouch for Moriarty's character. I have never known him to be dishonest about anything. Please release him into my custody, or at least into Uncle Augustus's."

Moriarty wanly smiled at me, but he looked as if he knew he was a condemned man in spite of my protests.

Sir Alastair patted my shoulder condescendingly. I was reminded of the odious Mr. Berwick. "My dear girl. We who are much older and wiser understand that you have a most commendable affection for a family servant, which blinds you to the possibility of his guilt. Please allow those of us who have more experience to guide you in matters of importance beyond your ability to grasp."

The only thing I wanted to grasp at that moment was his nose. And then I wanted to give it a violent twist. I recognized in Sir Alastair that most lamentable, yet common, attribute possessed by men of large responsibility and little ability—the desire to protect one's authority at all costs, no matter how injurious it may be to others, as well as the inability to let go of a bad idea.

"My dear Sir Alastair," I said through gritted teeth. "Please allow this young and inexperienced girl to aid you in recognizing the danger you will face when you suffer public humiliation for accusing the wrong person."

Sir Alastair's face turned puce. "Take him away."

Moriarty struggled anew as the government men dragged him off. Then, with a surprising turn of strength, he threw off his captors and bolted through the front door.

Chapter Twenty-one

In Which a Butler Reappears

IT IS A HEAVY BURDEN when one is responsible for the safe return of one's dearest friend, the national security of Mother England, and proving the innocence of one's butler. It is also a circumstance that one hopes will occur only once in one's lifetime. In this case, such an eventuality seemed very likely, since the collection of strange events we were experiencing could never be duplicated. Of that, at least, I was sure.

As our hansom cab bumped over cobbled streets on the way to the docks, Uncle Augustus ventured to speak to me. "Petronella, my dearest niece —"

"Your only niece, you mean," I interrupted. I was still in high dudgeon over Sir Alastair's condescending manner and his arrest of Moriarty.

Uncle sighed. "Yes, you are my only niece and therefore all that much more precious to me. However, I am not about to be the victim of your temper or your penchant for interrupting. We are on the same side, if you remember."

Anger sparked within my bosom for a moment more. Then a sense of the fairness of what Uncle Augustus said seeped in, and I could not remain angry, at least not with him. Sir Alastair was another matter. "I'm sorry, Uncle. I should not have spoken to you so. But I must say that Chumpy, as you call him, will rue the day he crossed Petronella Eunice Arbuthnot."

"Very well. The best way to get your revenge, dear niece, is to prove Chumpy wrong."

"And how do we propose to do that? This last note turns everything on its ear. How can we be sure of what anything is anymore?"

"Elimination. We narrowed down the possible source of the Colombian insects, and now we narrow down the ship they came from," said Uncle Augustus.

"Good plan," I said.

In the pearly dawn light subdued by thinning fog, I saw his fingers play with a bit of waxed paper protruding from his book. I looked away, unwilling to witness Uncle breakfasting. At least I'd provided for myself, having learned a valuable lesson about provisions and adventuring. In my pocket resided a tasty ham sandwich ready for any emergency requiring sustenance.

"Do you think the dame and generalissimo and Jane will be on the ship that brought the insects?" I asked, yawning. I had been awake for nearly twenty-four hours and the rocking of the hansom cab acted as a soporific. I could scarcely keep my eyes open.

Uncle, however, seemed wide awake and energetic. He said, "Very good observation, that. It is my belief that the ship in question is precisely where they are. They could scarcely be kept at the Savoy."

I yawned again and leaned my head back against the squabs, preparing to nap until we reached the docks. "My thoughts as well," I murmured. Then my eyes flew open. "Goodness gracious! Is that a head?"

"Eh, what?" said Uncle.

The top of a roundish object bobbed just outside my window. In the previously mentioned pearly dawn light, the object was only just discernible as a head. However, as I watched in fascination, I realized that the head could not accurately be described as bobbing. Bobbing involved more of a sharp ascension accompanied by a sharp descent. The action of this head consisted of smoother movements, which could not actually be described as a bob. It was almost as if the body attached to the head were gliding.

"Moriarty!" I exclaimed. I threw open the cab door, and my esteemed butler leaped inside.

"My word, man. What are you doing here?" asked Uncle Augustus.

Moriarty seated himself next to Uncle Augustus and straightened his shirt front and tie. "I thought it my duty to assist Miss Arbuthnot and yourself, Mr. Percival, and I could not do so from a prison cell. Besides, I wish to prove my innocence."

"Capital idea," I said. For some reason Moriarty's presence gave me much more confidence. Additionally, I was not loath to put one over on Sir Alastair.

Uncle Augustus frowned. "I'm afraid you have placed us in somewhat of an ethical dilemma," he said. "We are law-abiding citizens and you were lawfully arrested. We shall have to detour and return you to the authorities."

"Uncle Augustus!"

Moriarty nodded thoughtfully. "I understand your concern, sir. And I should do the same in your shoes. However, I am in possession of some vital information that precludes my returning to the authorities until I have acted upon it, and I presume that you will feel the same."

Chapter Twenty-Two

In Which a Star Is Found

I HAD ALWAYS THOUGHT OF the Thames as a quiet river. When one punts on the upper Thames, one hears only a bit of sloshing, with the occasional splash when some unfortunate punter falls in. Then there might also be a bit of shouting. Such an occurrence leaves one feeling smug that one is safe and dry; however, for the most part, the upper Thames is a prime example of the maxim that still waters run silent and deep.

The docks in London are another matter altogether.

When James had said that the *Star* and the *Constanza* were at the Royal Albert Dock, I imagined a collection of picturesque wooden piles and planks such as those where punts are tied up, only larger and perhaps encased quaintly in moss. I was unprepared for the complexity of the dock system, with the warehouses and locks and boats in all sizes and shapes and an extraordinary amount of loading and unloading being done.

I was also unprepared for the noise. Laborers shouted, sea birds cried, winches ground, and water slapped against the hulls of hundreds of ships—even at five in the morning. In fact, it looked as if the dockworkers never slept. If Uncle had thought that his strolling along the docks at this time of the morning might be conspicuous, he was sorely mistaken. So much bedlam was taking place that one would have had to run screaming, naked and on fire, through the crowds to attract attention, something I was not at all prepared to do.

Uncle, Moriarty, and I stood, daunted as we stared down the rows of vessels. Holding the piece of paper on which James had written the numbers of the berths where the *Star* and the *Constanza* were docked, Uncle Augustus started walking and counting. Moriarty and I followed.

"What was the information you wished to share?" I asked my butler.

"Only that I found footprints leading from the house to a tree and a set of bicycle tire tracks that led out from the tree to the road," said Moriarty.

"So, the person who delivered the ransom note for five thousand pounds came by bicycle. Very good, Moriarty. We shall tell Uncle Augustus."

We hurried after my uncle, still weaving his way down the dock. Every once in a while I noticed Uncle's fingers dart into the air or toward a pile of cargo and presumed that Uncle was breakfasting. I patted my pocket containing the ham sandwich.

While Uncle counted, I studied the name of each ship that we passed. Somewhere on one of them, if our summations were correct, were my dearest Jane and the dame and generalissimo. Tears gathered in my eyes as I worried about my bosom friend. Was she frightened or hungry or cold? I suppose I should have been worried about the generalissimo and dame and England's supremacy on the high seas as well, but I was tired and a bit frightened myself.

The thought of Jane, most naturally, brought additional thoughts of James, and my longing for him surprised me by its strength. I remembered how, only hours earlier, I had studied his manly profile, which was silhouetted in the dark carriage against the gaslit window. I pictured his broad shoulders and firm chin and could almost smell the perfume of his brilliantined hair. My heart beat a quick tattoo, rather in the manner of the drummers in the King's Guard as they changed watches at Buckingham Palace.

I had to admit that throughout this escapade, James had behaved with a great deal more fortitude than I would have thought possible, which only made him that much more attractive. However, I also had to admit that James had paid no more attention to me than he had when I was five years old. I sighed and realized that thoughts of James had prevented me from noticing the ships we were passing. So much so, in fact, that I bumped into Uncle Augustus when he stopped abruptly.

"Did you see one of the ships we seek?" I asked.

"No, but I did find this." Uncle opened his hand. In it was a Tou-eh-mah-mah butterfly. Its wings quivered, then waved gracefully up and down. It took off, fluttering erratically down the dock.

Uncle, Moriarty, and I glanced at each other in astonishment. Then we sprinted after the butterfly. I soon lost sight of the insect, but Uncle Augustus seemed to see it quite clearly and darted down the dock as erratically as the butterfly. Moriarty and I were left to pound along behind him as best we could, although, to be honest, Moriarty glided and I pounded.

Ahead of us, Uncle slid to a halt, his fingers flashing in and out of stacks of logs next to a large, enclosed wagon. Was Uncle so famished he could not help but stop to feast? To my amazement, though, he didn't seem to be eating. Instead, he pulled out a handkerchief and deposited whatever he had caught into the fabric's recesses. He knotted the corners of the handkerchief together and dropped it into his

149

coat pocket. Only then did he deftly snag a few flitting creatures and pop them into his mouth. I was close enough to
hear a crunch or two as he chewed, but I was too interested
in what he had found to be as thoroughly revolted as I would
have been at another time.

Moriarty, however, could not help a small yelp of amazement. It was the first time I had known Moriarty to lose his
composure, and I supposed we should have to inform him of
my guardian's altered state, since it did not appear that Uncle would be cured anytime soon. Hopefully, Moriarty would
not give notice. It is so difficult to find good servants these
days.

"Dear Uncle, what did you put in the handkerchief?" I
asked.

Uncle Augustus barely paid attention to what I said as he
stared at the ship adjacent to the stacks of logs trailing
strands of cinnamon-colored bark. He answered, but he
sounded as if his consciousness was elsewhere. "Tou-eh-
mah-mah insects — as evidence."

"From the logs? Does that mean that these logs are from
Tou-eh-mah-mah Island?" I asked.

"It does seem likely," answered Uncle, brow furrowed in
thought. "And I would think they came from that ship there,
but it is not named the *Star* or the *Constanza*. The name on
the prow is *Estrella*."

Moriarty coughed, then cleared his throat. "I do not wish to seem to act beyond my position, but permit me to give you some small information in my possession. In Spanish, *estrella* means 'star.'"

"Then why didn't the dock master tell us the ship was the *Estrella*?" asked Uncle.

My eyes narrowed as I pondered possibilities. I said, "If my deductions are accurate, I do believe the dock master is trying to shield the kidnappers by misleading us over the name of the ship. Traitorous fiend. Do you think he was bribed?"

"You are most likely all too correct, dear niece," said Uncle Augustus. "Since the names are so similar, and the insects so abundant among the logs, we do not need to search further. The kidnappers are on that ship. Now we just need a good plan to get on board."

Chapter Twenty-three

In Which a Blood-Encrusted
Medal Is Discovered

WHEN ONE HEARS THE WORD *plan* in conjunction with actions one is about to engage in, one might expect to find comfort in said word. It connotes care in future proceedings, and *care* connotes safety for those occupied in carrying out whatever has been devised. However, insect eating by the planner does not inspire confidence. Therefore, it was with great misgivings that I listened to Uncle's plan and agreed to participate. The only thing that gave me comfort was that Moriarty was also part of the arrangement, and I trusted his good sense to carry the day or restrain Uncle, whichever seemed necessary at the moment.

There was no one in sight on the ship, but even as we waited, the activity on the dock seemed to increase with the rising of the sun. We decided that we must put our plan in motion without delay.

Moriarty's role was to discard his butler's jacket, remove his shirt collar, and roll up the sleeves of his white shirt. Then he was to heave onto his shoulder a wooden box that he garnered from an adjoining part of the dock and walk up the gangplank as if he were loading the ship. I just hoped no one noticed the knife-edge crease to his trousers or the shine to his shoes, which was rumored to be the result of rubbing with champagne—from my cellar, no doubt. Once on board, my esteemed butler was to snoop. If he found something, he was to alert me.

I would be waiting on the dock in case of such a contingency. Once alerted, I would contact the nearest bobby, one of whom I could see farther down the dock, swinging his nightstick. The trick was to not catch the bobby's attention until after our plan was in motion, or he might feel we were breaking and entering unlawfully and try to stop us. Technically, we were bending the law somewhat by boarding the ship without permission, but we assumed that if we saved the generalissimo and the dame and perhaps Jane, such a breach of jurisprudence would most likely be forgiven.

Uncle's part in our little drama was a bit more hazy in my mind. He, too, was supposed to board the ship, but from the other side. How I was not sure, but it had something to do with the anchor chain, or a rope, or some such thing. It also included Uncle's newfound ability to climb, which is how he had gotten atop Lord Nelson's Column the previous evening. I watched, somewhat puzzled, as Uncle pushed off from the dock in one of the little rowboats called lighters, which were used to load and unload ships. Uncle had a spot of trouble with the oars at first. He rowed in a circle for several strokes, and then found his rhythm and neatly slipped the lighter around the nether end of the ship.

I was left standing on the dock, holding Moriarty's butler jacket and thinking that although Uncle and Moriarty might not seem conspicuous on a dock at five-thirty in the morning, I did. There weren't any other females that I could see. Normally, one might expect to spot a few ladies preparing to board ships as passengers even this early in the morning, since many cargo ships had passenger cabins, and everyone knew that ships departed at the most awfully inconvenient times. But, as I already mentioned, I was the only person of a female physique anywhere in the vicinity. I was surprised at how vulnerable such a position made me feel. I only hoped the bobby did not think it necessary to check up on me before I was signaled by Moriarty or Uncle.

Trying to look as if I belonged on a dock, I busied myself with the enclosed wagon next to the stack of Tou-eh-mah-

mah Island logs. It seemed to be a sturdy wooden wagon very like those I had seen in London and along the country roads near my estate, which were commonly used to haul whatever needed hauling. Could this be the vehicle that had transported the dame and generalissimo? The back was open, and I could see several logs piled inside as if whoever owned the wagon was going to deliver them somewhere. As I moved to one side of the opening, the morning sun shone inside. Something glinted.

I peered between the logs. Just visible was a bit of faceted, glimmering red surrounded by patterned gold. The opening in the logs was too small even for my hand. But by pushing and pulling them, I was able to widen the opening ever so slightly and ease my fingertips between the logs and retrieve the glinting object.

When I opened my fingers, there, lying on my palm and catching the rays of the sun, was one of Generalissimo Reyes-Cardoza's medals — its ruby and gold splendor slightly dulled on one side by dried blood.

Chapter Twenty-four

In Which a Ship Is Boarded

TO HAVE ONE'S GUESTS KIDNAPPED and one's bosom friend disappear is serious enough in itself. But the addition of dried blood on a medal into the mix is enough to give one pause. In that pause one is forced to solemnly reflect that what one saw as only a possibility for injury was most likely a fact. Blood is not usually present on the medals of Panamanian generalissimos unless someone has been maimed.

I scanned the ship for any sign of my avuncular relative or my butler. Nothing. It being late spring, the sun was now well up in the sky. It had been quite some time since my partners in crime had boarded the ship. At least one of them should have signaled me by now. Panic arose in my breast. To have persons kidnapped whom one does not know at all well was one thing, but to have one's own uncle and butler, not to mention one's bosom friend, disappear was another cup of custard altogether. It was time to go for the bobby.

It has been asked, and rightly so in my opinion, "Where is a bobby when you need one?" The member of the police force who had been down the dock, nonchalantly swinging his nightstick, was nowhere to be seen. So much for Uncle's plan. Now what was I to do?

I stood indecisively next to the wagon, gripping the generalissimo's medal in my hand until its gold points dug into my palm. By now, nearly six in the morning, even more dockworkers bustled about their business loading and unloading nearby ships. Lighters and lorries floated or trundled about purposefully, while the *Estrella* remained suspiciously devoid of activity. People of one sort or another were everywhere, but not on that ship, at least not where one could see them.

I thought that perhaps I could persuade someone on the docks to board the ship with me and help me search. The generalissimo's medal might convince them that I was not insane. But then I remembered that it seemed that the dock master had purposely given us incorrect information. I wondered how deeply he was involved with the kidnappers and if their influence extended to the dockworkers. Some of them might be under instruction to watch the ship and prevent escape. All those bustling, hustling persons suddenly seemed sinister.

I wondered where James was with his band of merry Home Office employees. Surely he should have been here by now. I scanned the dock for some sign of his handsome visage, feeling like one of the damsels in distress one reads about in Arthurian legend. Where was my Sir Galahad? Gone the way of the bobby, for all I knew, having a spot of tea somewhere cozy.

Feeling the combined Arbuthnot and Percival resolve rise to the occasion, I breathed in and squared my shoulders. It was up to me to find Uncle and Moriarty and the generalissimo and the dame, and my dear friend Jane.

It was a simple matter to sprint lightly up the gangplank and onto the ship. No one tried to stop me. Nor did they stop me from sneaking silently up the stairs leading to the bridge, which, to my relief, was empty. I must admit that although my ancestry stiffened my spine, my heart was all my own and on the edge of paralyzing fear. Even so, I forged on.

From the bridge I could see the hatch leading to the hold, but no other way to go into the lower regions of the ship. I had seen some metal doors that probably led to cabins below the bridge. It was my guess that if the victims were being held, it would be in one of the cabins on the side of the ship facing away from the dock. Calling upon skills honed to perfection by my attempts to elude governesses, I crept down the stairs I had just ascended.

The second door opened, and three burly sailors exited, walking away from me. I slipped around and under the stairs in a trice, my unruly heart hammering. They spoke in fluid tones that I thought sounded like Spanish. I wished I had paid more attention to Miss Spackering's Spanish lessons. If I'd known that language would be of use for the purposes of espionage instead of small talk in the drawing room, I might have applied myself to my lessons more diligently. Only a few of the sailors' words made sense to me, and they all had to do with food and money. Of course, they were being sent to buy breakfast, and quite a bit of it, from what I could decipher. I heaved a sigh of relief. That meant at least three of the crew would be gone for a while.

When the sailors had rounded the corner and were out of sight, I eased along the wall in the direction of the first cabin, careful to keep my head below the round windows. Pressing my ear to the metal door, I listened. All was quiet within, although I thought I could hear a puzzling thrumming as well as feeling it through the soles of my shoes. I couldn't place the source of the thrumming, but it was definitely not human. Surely the metal would have reverberated if anyone was speaking. I could only suppose that the cabin was empty.

Sidling toward the door from which the sailors had exited, my aforementioned unruly heart leaped into my throat as I heard voices coming from inside the second cabin. This time, when I pressed my ear to the door, I could clearly hear a heated discussion taking place.

Chapter Twenty-five

In Which Much Is Overheard

I HAVE LEARNED THAT ONE must, when conducting espionage, be open to having one's assumptions challenged. In this case—ear pressed to door, expecting to hear the voices of known victims and kidnappers—I had my assumptions shattered.

Uncle's voice said, "Well, Don Salas, you have captured everyone, including Miss Sinclair. What have you done with her?"

A deep male voice with a thick Spanish accent, undoubtedly Don Hernando Salas, answered, "That, Mr. Percival, you shall never know. If your stupid Scotland Yard inspector could not find Pedro last night, no one shall find Miss Sinclair, either."

Another accented male voice chimed in. "Pity we had to

hide her so quickly. She is *muy bonita*. Too bad she proved to be more trouble than we cared to deal with."

If Jane was not there, where was she? My brow furrowed. The second voice sounded familiar. Where had I heard it before?

I forgot the question as another familiar voice demanded, "You must let us go. You have taken on more than you know. My husband will have the Hussars after you."

Great-Aunt Theophilia? What was she doing here?

"My mother's right, you know. Father will go to the ends of the earth to revenge any wrongs done to his girls."

"Too right," said a little voice.

Crimea? Boeotia? I longed to peek into the window but knew that if I did, I should be spotted.

Harsh laughter greeted these pronouncements. "Whatever we do to you will serve you right for sneaking into my suite at the Savoy," said Don Hernando Salas. "You delude yourselves if you believe that anything you say will make any difference to your fate."

"What about this?" said someone who sounded just like Aunt Cordelia, followed by a loud thump and a shout of pain.

"Vicious woman. Tie her feet to her chair," Don Hernando Salas said as if through clenched teeth.

I stifled a chuckle as I imagined Aunt Cordelia kicking Don Hernando Salas.

There was another thump and Pedro cried out. Then sounds of a struggle.

"She is tied," said Pedro. "Is my eye black?"

Were all my relations there? Had they discussed the clues and come to the same conclusion that Uncle, James, and I had been captured and brought here? Where was James?

"You are making a grave mistake if you think that by kidnapping us you can do your country any good. Our *revolucion*'s success is assured." The speaker could only be Generalissimo Reyes-Cardoza.

Then the ringing tones of Dame Carruthers caused the cabin door to vibrate as she proclaimed, "Mother England shall triumph. Your puny efforts will make no difference. You will only cause your own motherland much embarrassment."

Don Hernando Salas responded, "Ah, but we have another part of our plan besides simple kidnapping—one much more effective and devastating to you smug Englishmen. We shall, in fact, be putting it into motion as soon as the crew arrives with the provisions we need. I do not think your country has the means to combat an epidemic of yellow fever and malaria. It will be a just retribution for meddling in our affairs."

I started with surprise. So the sailors' conversation I had overheard was not about breakfast, but about provisions. And kidnapping was not the only string to their bow. James had been right in thinking that the abductions were a diversion to mask a different agenda. Now it seemed they had devised a ghastly threat. I suppose putting down a rebellion is commendable when your viewpoint is from that of the country seeking to halt a colony's liberation. Just look at what had happened with the American colonies. Most distressing. But to threaten England with tropical diseases was unconscionable. And how were they to carry out such a threat?

My attention was brought sharply back to the present as Don Hernando said, "The addition of several members of the British aristocracy to our cargo will only increase our bargaining power. Thank you for making it so easy to capture you. I'm afraid accommodations will be rather crowded, though. We were only counting on two."

Then he said, "Pedro, check the ropes and make sure they are tight. We must make ready for our journey along the Thames and the depositing of our cargo along the way."

There was a bit of noise as if people were standing and moving about. I, too, stood, wondering what to do. If Don

Hernando and Pedro left the cabin, they would certainly find me. Additionally, whatever I did, it had to be before the crew returned, or they could carry out their horrific plan.

As I considered what few options I had, my fingers played with the folds of Moriarty's coat and found a small, hard object. I smiled. Of course. I had the perfect weapon.

Chapter Twenty-six

In Which a Plan Is Perpetrated

WHEN ONE HAS THOUGHT OF the perfect plan and has but split seconds to execute it, one prefers not to consider consequences, since the consideration of consequences may lead to hesitation, and he or she who hesitates is often lost. Consequences are those often nasty effects that follow decisions or actions, rather like the aftershocks of an earthquake. I have heard it said that one may choose one's actions, but one may not always choose the results. However, in this case I took care to ensure that the outcome of my perfect plan would be inimitably satisfactory.

My scheme required but three items: two lengths of rope, found conveniently wrapped around the large cleats on the deck, and the object I had located in Moriarty's coat pocket — the Vile Vial. The rope I formed into loops, one on the end of

each rope and knotted securely with a knot that Miss Spackering had taught me while I was embroidering a tea cosy.
The Vile Vial, however, was the crowning glory of my plan.

I tied my handkerchief to cover my nose and mouth. Then
I eased open the cabin door, wincing as it creaked a bit, and
threw down the unstoppered glass Vile Vial, which splin-
tered on the metal floor of the cabin as I slammed the door
shut and leaned against it with all my might.

Screams echoed from inside the cabin. Oh, well. It was
for their own good.

I managed to hold down the door handle for a few seconds, which I was sure was enough to allow Moriarty's po-
tent potion to take full effect. Don Hernando Salas and
Pedro (I assumed it was they) lunged against the door once
and it nearly gave way. But the next lunge was weaker than
the one before, and the one after that was more like a bump
than a lunge. Even the screaming of my beloved relations
died to a mere mumble. I hoped they would forgive me eventually.

I threw open the door. As Don Hernando and then Pedro
stumbled out, reeling from the effects of the Vile Vial, I flung
a loop of rope over each in turn, pulled tight, and then used
the rest of the rope to secure feet and hands. Neither one
had the strength to do more than wriggle a bit after taking
the full force of the Vile Vial, being closest to the door when

it broke. I was grateful for the sea breeze that saved me from having to breathe any of the fumes. In a trice, both kidnappers were trussed up like the swine they were. Miss Spackering would have been proud of my knots.

I gloated over the results of my plan for only a moment before I rushed to help the other inhabitants of the cabin. From the baleful looks they gave me as I entered—looks that would have been murderous if the lookers had not been coughing and wheezing and attempting not to vomit—I could tell that my estimable relatives and the other victims might not appreciate my cleverness to the extent that I did. Even after at least a minute of fresh air circulating about the cabin, the fumes were enough to make my eyes water, so that I could barely see the bonds that tied the victims to chairs and bunks. I decided that discretion was the better part of valor and untied only Moriarty, who seemed the least affected, probably because he had built up an immunity to his own concoction, having been exposed to it quite recently.

Once my butler was free, I asked through my handkerchief, "Moriarty, would you do me the favor of untying everyone while I look for someone who has the authority to arrest the kidnappers?" I edged toward the door of the cabin in order to be away as quickly as possible lest one of the victims should recover enough to take revenge once untied.

"Yes, miss," gasped Moriarty.

"And don't let the kidnappers escape." Tearing off the handkerchief, I whirled away, sprinting around to the gangplank and onto the dock, only to run smack into James's chest. I considered staying comfortably splayed out against him, but he grasped my shoulders and held me at arm's length.

"Wherever have you been?" he shouted. "We've been looking all over the *Constanza* for you. I've been so worried. First Jane and then you." His voice caught.

I goggled at him. Could he care for me even the least bit? His concern seemed to indicate that such might be the case. Then I realized that he blamed me for his inability to find me, and my temper flared.

I shouted back, "And where have you been? I've had to capture the kidnappers and rescue everyone all by myself. You could have been a great help, but no, you had to ignore all the clues and—"

"You did what?" he shouted even louder.

I pulled from his grasp and pointed to the stacks of logs with butterflies flitting about them. In the same voice I would use with a two-year-old, I said, "Look at the Tou-eh-mah-mah butterflies and the logs. Look at the ship they came from. Put the two together and *voilà*, we have kidnappers and victims on that very ship."

James chose to ignore my tone of voice. "You didn't board the ship by yourself, did you?" he asked accusingly.

169

"Rather," I answered. "There was no one else to save everyone." I hoped that he would be stung by my sarcasm, but it did not seem to affect him in the least.

"You should have waited for us." He indicated at least twenty government personnel, all nearly identical to each other, who ranged behind him. One of them waved at me. I waved back.

"Halloo! Halloo there!"

Both James and I turned to view Sir Alastair clambering out of a carriage and scuttling toward us, followed by Inspector Higginbotham and Sergeant Crumple hauling Georgie Grimsley, who looked much the worse for wear, between them.

Gasping for air from his exertions, Sir Alastair stopped in front of James and me. "I do hope I've caught you in time before you do anything foolish to upset international relations, such as barging onto other people's boats. We've caught the kidnapper."

"Georgie Grimsley?" James and I said together in disbelief.

Sir Alastair beamed at the two of us. "Yes. Without a doubt. The clues all point to him. He was at the party. He was at Miss Arbuthnot's shortly after the second note arrived. He was in London yesterday, and he was hanging about the place where the last note demanded the delivery of the five thousand pounds. The only problem is that he won't tell us where the generalissimo and the dame are. Says he doesn't know or some such rot. I thought that perhaps you could persuade him to do his patriotic duty and confess."

"I didn't kidnap anyone, and I don't know where anyone is. All I did was send that stupid note about the five thousand pounds because I was rejected by Miss Arbuthnot," whined Georgie.

My mind reeled. "You did what? You worm." I turned to Sir Alastair. "But it is true, he doesn't know anything else, and he is not the kidnapper," I said. "Because the kidnappers are all tied up on that ship and being watched over by Moriarty, the generalissimo and the dame, and most of my relations."

"You didn't tell me about your relations," accused James.

"You didn't ask," I retorted. I turned to Sir Alastair, "Now, you'd better hurry and relieve poor Moriarty of guard duty."

Sir Alastair motioned to the government personnel to follow him and marched up the gangplank. Inspector Higginbotham and Sergeant Crumple stood on the dock hanging on to Georgie as if loath to let him go.

James started after Sir Alastair. Then he turned slowly toward me. "You didn't mention Jane. Was she not on the ship with the others?"

I shook my head sorrowfully. "No. She was not."

Chapter Twenty-seven

In Which a Door Is Opened

AFTER FOILING A DESPERATE CRIMINAL, one would expect to feel just the least bit exhilarated. I did not. I felt a complete failure. Part of the depression, I'm sure, came from not sleeping for over twenty-four hours, but a great deal more of it came from having failed to find my friend.

"Where could she be?" asked James. He seemed to be in as great a despair as I was.

Inspector Higginbotham and Sergeant Crumple both turned to glare at Georgie Grimsley, who whimpered, "I don't know anything, I say. I don't know how to find her, either."

His words triggered a memory of Don Hernando Salas saying, "If your stupid Scotland Yard inspector could not find Pedro last night, no one shall find Miss Sinclair, either."

"We must go to Trafalgar Square," I said.

"What? This is no time to be sightseeing," blustered Inspector Higginbotham.

"I still fink it's 'im wot's pinched the girl," complained Sergeant Crumple, pointing to Georgie. James and I ignored him.

"You're on to something?" James asked me.

"I think so," I answered.

He grabbed my hand and pulled me toward Sir Alastair's carriage. "Then let's be off."

As we climbed in the carriage, leaving Inspector Higginbotham, Sergeant Crumple, and Georgie Grimsley staring after us, James shouted up to the driver, "Trafalgar Square, and there's a hundred extra quid if you're quick about it."

When the carriage halted, we climbed somewhat gingerly out at nearly the same place I had stood the night before, opposite Nelson's Column.

We blinked owlishly in the early-morning sunlight as we gazed at the contents of Trafalgar Square. The fog was gone. The sun illuminated the plinths, all but one of which had statues atop them. There was Nelson's Column in all its glory. There were the fountains that were supposed to keep mobs from getting out of control. Where could Pedro have hidden in all this open space? I walked forward to gain a different viewpoint, but saw nothing unusual. I backed up. What was that? There, on the southeast corner, stood a small stone-and-glass building no bigger than a closet. The odd structure even had a faceted glass ball that seemed to be a light fixture sitting atop it. The whole structure looked something like a squat lamppost. Londoners strode past it without giving it a glance, but I could not tear my eyes away.

"What is that?" I pointed toward the little building.

"Oh, don't you know? It's the world's smallest police station. There is only room for one officer in there, and the light on top is said to come from Nelson's flagship, the *Victory*." James continued scanning the square.

I tugged on his sleeve. "Let's go look."

"We are looking."

Now, I have often thought that James is the most adorable man I have ever known, but he can be maddening at times. He has flashes of insight that lead one to believe in his intellectual prowess, but at other times he is positively imbecilic. I started off in the direction of the tiny police station.

"Where are you going?" James sprinted after me.

"To that police station. It's the only place Jane could be. That kidnapper could easily have hidden in there, since the police might not have manned it in the middle of the night, and I heard Don Hernando Salas say that if we could not find where Pedro had hidden last night, we would not find Jane," I explained reasonably, and kept on walking. James followed, muttering.

When I reached the police station, I pulled on its glass-paned door only to find it locked. I tugged harder, but it would not budge. I pressed my face against the glass, but there was not enough light to see to the very bottom, so I resumed rattling the door. I could have sworn it budged the tiniest bit.

James peered in but evidently did not see anything more than I had. "I think you're quite insane. We should look in one of the nearby shops. Much more logical," said James.

When I didn't answer, he said, "Fine then, do as you please. I shall investigate the shops myself." He left.

"Here, what do you think you're doing, miss?"

I turned to see a bobby hurrying toward me. He pointed his nightstick at me and asked again, "What do you think you're up to, messing with my station?"

"Rescuing my friend," I answered.

"And what friend would that be?" he asked, rocking back on his heels. "If you're in trouble, you should go to the main station that's open all night. This one isn't manned until seven each morning, and I'm the one that's manning it now."

"Then would you please be so good as to open it? My friend Jane is inside."

He rolled his eyes. "Now what would she be doing in a place like that?"

"Kidnappers put her there," I answered with equanimity. I was seething with impatience, but I held my tongue. I'd met the bobby's like before. I knew that if I pushed, he'd just dig in his heels harder and I'd never find Jane.

"Kidnappers, is it? Fine tale, that."

"Yes, it is. When are you going to be on duty so I can tell you about it?" I asked.

He puffed out his chest. "I'm on duty now. You can tell me, miss."

"But when are you going to be inside your station? You do have the key, don't you? How do I know you're not just posing as a bobby?"

He sighed and took out a ring of keys from his pocket, slipped one of the keys into the lock, and opened the door. Out rolled Jane, tied up in a sack with only her eyes showing. They were quite large and filled with tears. I hoped they were tears of relief.

"Well, I never," said the bobby.

I gently released the rope that tied the sack. The knots were not nearly as tidy as the ones Miss Spackering had taught me, exhibiting a shocking lack of professionalism on Pedro's part, and were therefore much more easily undone. "Oh, Jane. What have they done to you?"

She mumbled something, but I could not hear because of the gag in her mouth. I undid that as well.

The bobby and I raised her to a standing position, but she collapsed, and we had to set her down on the stone wall next to the police station.

I sat next to her and took her hand in mine. "Are you all right?" I asked as I handed her a rather crumpled handkerchief that I unwound from my somewhat squashed ham sandwich.

She sniffed and blew her nose into the handkerchief. "Yes, thank you. I've been wanting to do that all night."

"Glad to oblige," I said. As the morning sun warmed my back, a lovely peace stole over me. Family, friends, and country were all safe. If only Uncle Augustus would take the antidote, all would be well and I could concentrate on a brilliant London season.

"Is that a ham sandwich?" Jane asked. "I'm rather hungry. Adventuring does that to one, doesn't it?"

At that moment James rushed across the square and knelt at Jane's feet. "Jane, dear. Are you all right?"

"Quite," she answered. She smiled at her brother but then looked longingly at the sandwich.

I handed it to her. "Adventuring does indeed make one hungry. I've become rather an expert in that area."

Chapter Twenty-eight

In Which Retribution Is Averted

EVEN WHEN ONE HAS RESCUED one's dearest friend, as well as several relations and other persons of consequence, in addition to the British economy and the Panamanian cause for liberty, there is still, forever and always, something that requires one's attention. That is, unless one is deceased, and I, fortunately, was not.

When Jane was finished with the ham sandwich and we had explained all that had transpired since we last met, I rose to my feet and held out my hand to her. "Dearest friend, do you feel up to a ride? We must return Sir Alastair's carriage and retrieve miscellaneous relations who are most likely without the means of retrieving themselves."

"Absolutely not, old prune. Jane is much too battered to

cavort about in a carriage. Give her time to collect herself," said James.

Jane grasped my hand and pulled herself up, albeit a bit shakily. Our eyes met, and we exchanged the silent message of friendship and the knowledge that men can be ever so silly regarding misconceptions of female intrepidity. She swallowed the last bite of ham sandwich and said, "Nonsense, James. I'm not some hothouse flower. Besides, aren't you the least bit curious about those you left at the docks?"

We turned to the bobby, who was standing open-mouthed near his minuscule police station, looking every bit as silly as James. I bent my head grandly in the bobby's direction. "Thank you for your good offices, sir. We truly appreciate your cooperation, and your country thanks you as well."

We nearly made it to the carriage before Jane and I burst into a fit of the giggles. The carriage had been driven by the alert driver nearer to the corner where the police station was located and where we were situated.

Jane turned back toward James. "Are you coming or not? Too tired, dear brother?"

At that, James leaped to his feet from where he had been sitting on the wall and strode forward to insert himself between Jane and myself. He took Jane's arm on one side, and my arm on his other. Did I delude myself, or did he hold my

179

arm close in a particularly warm manner? How was it that after all that had happened, I still tingled at his touch? I felt myself to have grown much older in the last few days, having changed in many ways from the girl whose coming-out party was foremost on her mind. For one thing, I now knew I was capable of more than I had thought possible and that my family, friends, and country mattered.

However, James could still make my heart flutter. It fluttered all the more when James pulled Jane and me closer still and exclaimed, "All for one and one for all!" We laughed rather giddily. Then he handed us into the carriage.

Before James entered, I heard him say, "Here's the promised hundred quid. Now we may return to the docks and Sir Alastair."

The driver answered, "Right, sir. And may Oi just say Oi'm 'appy to 'ave been of some small service in rescuin' the miss. Right bit of detective work that were."

"Right," said James, not admitting that it had been *my* right bit of detective work, for which I felt the slightest bit peeved. Then he swung himself into the carriage, and we were off once more, only not quite in such a harum-scarum manner as we had come.

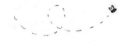

THE DOCKS WERE still abustle, but there were a few differences. Most of the Home Office personnel were absent, along with Don Hernando and Pedro, as were the inspector, sergeant, Georgie Grimsley, the dame, and the generalissimo. My relations stood about looking quite miserable, although Moriarty was in the act of serving them tea from a tea trolley he had somehow procured. He also had acquired cakes.

The most startling difference was the presence of Professor Lepworthy, in deep conversation with Sir Alastair, Uncle Augustus, and the remaining Home Office personnel.

"What is Professor Lepworthy doing here?" asked Jane as she alighted from the carriage.

"I have no idea," said James. "Perhaps he came because of the Tou-eh-mah-mah butterflies."

A light dawned in my weary brain. I remembered the strange sound on the ship. "No, not butterflies. The thrumming I heard. Mosquitoes. Yellow fever or malaria," I said.

"What are you talking about?" asked Jane.

"The yellow fever and malaria Don Hernando said he would unleash from the ship," I explained.

James said, "You mean that theory that Dr. Finlay and Dr. Gorgas have been putting about that mosquitoes carry those tropical diseases?" He proved once again that all of his muscles were magnificent, including those in his head.

I scurried toward Uncle, calling over my shoulder, "Precisely. Don Hernando threatened worse than a kidnapping. What would happen to London if a ship full of mosquitoes carrying tropical diseases was unleashed on an unsuspecting populace?"

Jane and James scurried after me. "Disaster," they said in unison.

As we approached Uncle Augustus, Professor Lepworthy—whose errant toupee was held firmly in place by a bowler hat—and Sir Alastair, we heard Sir Alastair protesting, "But it has not even been proven that mosquitoes carry disease. It is much more likely to be dirty linen."

"Yes, it has, Chumpy, old prune. Do listen to reason and exercise a bit of caution," said Uncle. "It is unfortunate that you sent your men onto the ship and they entered the hold, but at least we now know that the true cargo of this ship is vats and vats of mosquito larvae and that they are meant to decimate London once they are dumped in the Thames."

Professor Lepworthy added, "Yes, I'm sorry for your poor men. I expect they'll be in hospital within three or four days. However, their actions may have saved England by alerting us to the danger. The mosquitoes they brought out are indeed the *Stegomyia* and the *Anopheles,* which scientific researchers have proven to be the carriers of yellow fever and malaria. Most interesting. The *Anopheles* especially—it bites while standing on its head." Professor Lepworthy unfolded a piece of waxed paper, undoubtedly supplied by Uncle Augustus, who was still clutching *Insectile Creatures*. He studied whatever was deposited on it through a magnifying glass. "Definitely a *Stegomyia*."

Sir Alastair harrumphed. I could see he was waffling in his opinions and not quite sure what to do, so I decided to make a foray into political arbitration. "So good to see you here, Sir Alastair. You will know just what to tell the newspapers about how you saved England from certain death. It is a great comfort to know that a man of your stature will have the foresight to avert disaster through the latest scientific means."

Sir Alastair looked thoughtful. "I would look heroic, wouldn't I?" He turned to Professor Lepworthy. "And what exactly is the latest scientific method?"

Professor Lepworthy was busily engaged in examining the mosquitoes on the waxed paper, exclaiming particularly over the beauty of the *Stegomyia*. He said rather absently, "It's actually quite easy to kill these delicate creatures. All you have to do is spray them with kerosene. Then the film that settles on the water where the larvae reside also kills the larvae because they cannot breathe. Major Walter Reed has been killing them off by the millions in Havana using that method. Pity. They're such interesting creatures."

Uncle Augustus stepped forward. "I volunteer to go into the hold to do the spraying," he said with an eagerness that belied his motive.

"What, old boy? You'd put yourself at risk to save your country?" Sir Alastair was visibly affected by his friend's proposed sacrifice.

I, however, was under no illusion as to my uncle's goal in making such an offer. He was anticipating lunch. There was one problem. I said, "A grand idea, dear uncle. However, would you not be putting yourself at risk of succumbing to disease if you are bitten?"

Uncle Augustus's eager countenance fell under the onslaught of reason, much as Rome had fallen to the Gauls.

"Not likely. Not after what has happened to him," said Professor Lepworthy under his breath. He looked up from his study of the mosquitoes to find all our attention firmly directed toward him. He glanced from Uncle Augustus to me and then to Jane and James and finally to Sir Alastair. The expressions on our faces ranged from puzzlement on Sir Alastair's countenance to various stages of alarm. Professor Lepworthy could be referring only to the change that had been wrought on Uncle Augustus. I shuddered to think what Sir Alastair would think of that. It would be the ruination of Uncle's reputation—and mine.

When the professor looked in my direction, I shook my head in negation and warning. So did Uncle Augustus, Jane, and James as he scanned their visages. Jane raised one finger to her lips.

"Oh," said Professor Lepworthy as he registered our condemnation of revealing certain information. "No?"

We all shook our heads more vigorously.

"Oh, what? No, what?" demanded Sir Alastair acerbically, clearly taking umbrage at our silent code.

Professor Lepworthy seemed to consider what to do for a moment, then withdrew another bit of waxed paper from his pocket and unfolded it, holding it before us. He said, "Observe the Tou-eh-mah-mah butterfly and beetle that I captured near the logs that have been unloaded from the *Estrella*. These insects are known to feast on the *Stegomyia* and the *Anopheles* mosquitoes. Once the mosquitoes have been eaten, the beetles produce a serum that provides a natural immunity to malaria and yellow fever. Ingesting such insects is one way known to aboriginal tribes of acquiring immunity, much like what happens to those who have had the diseases and become immune to them." He nodded meaningfully at Uncle Augustus, who suddenly seemed much happier—overjoyed, in fact.

"Are you suggesting we eat those insects in order to acquire immunity? Quite disgusting and . . . and un-British," said Sir Alastair. "Besides, what does it have to do with you, Augustus?"

Uncle Augustus turned toward the home secretary. "I think the professor was merely reminding me that over the course of my lifetime, and, er, certain events, I have acquired a natural immunity to malaria and yellow fever. Am I correct in making such an assumption?" Uncle turned toward Professor Lepworthy, who nodded vigorously.

"Quite so," said the professor.

"I had no idea you'd been through such an ordeal," said Sir Alastair. "That does rather change my view of your sacrifice on behalf of Mother England. Not nearly so dangerous, what?"

"Precisely," said Uncle. "Therefore, I suggest I board the *Estrella* and ascertain the best procedure to, um, dispatch the mosquitoes while you send your men for spraying equipment and kerosene."

"Very good," said Sir Alastair. He immediately gathered his remaining government men and was soon in conversation with them.

"And now, if you'll excuse me," said Uncle Augustus to Jane, James, Professor Lepworthy, and me as he patted *Insectile Creatures* with great satisfaction. "I have a little matter to attend to." With that he sauntered off toward the *Estrella*,

186

with a spring in his step that anticipated the culinary delights awaiting him.

"He can't mean to . . ." said Jane.

"How many thousands of them are there?" asked James.

"Millions, more than likely," answered Professor Lepworthy.

"Bravo, Uncle Augustus," I said. I burst into laughter and was quickly joined by the others, all except Sir Alastair, who looked as if he thought himself transported to Bedlam.

Chapter Twenty-nine

In Which a Cure Is Possible

WHEN ONE HAS CAUSE TO celebrate, one should do so. However, in order to celebrate to the fullest, one must not be merely one. One must have friends who feel some investment in the cause for celebration. Such was the case the next noon as Uncle Augustus and I welcomed Jane and James to a celebratory nuncheon on the south lawn.

I enjoyed the sumptuous repast, especially after the deprivations of the previous few days, as did Jane. James, of course, always has a hearty appetite. However, in spite of the variety and abundance of foodstuffs present, Uncle seemed content merely to watch us as we partook of the delicacies on the table, his hands folded over his rounded tummy, clearly still satiated by his feast on the ship the day before. We discussed our adventures, filling each other in on the events that had taken place when we were apart. We were just describing to Uncle how we had found Jane, when Moriarty approached.

As Moriarty glided across the lawn holding aloft his ubiquitous silver tray, we saw Professor Lepworthy, toupee slipping and sliding on his shining pate, shambling along behind clutching a slender-necked amber bottle and an envelope.

"Professor Maximus Lepworthy," announced Moriarty.

Uncle Augustus leaped to his feet and shook the professor's hand. "My good man. How pleased I am to see you. Won't you join us? There's plenty of room. Moriarty, please see to setting another place."

"As good as done, sir," said Moriarty, and from his silver tray he produced the necessary cutlery and china, arranging them into a setting next to Uncle Augustus's place. Then he snapped his fingers, and a footman brought along another chair.

It suddenly occurred to me that Moriarty had shared in our adventures as much as anyone, and although he was of the servant class, we owed him a great deal. "Would you care to join us as well, Moriarty? We should be happy to include you after all you have done for us, old friend," I said. Out of the corner of my eye I saw the footman's mouth fall open at my suggestion. However, Uncle Augustus, Jane, and James all nodded approvingly.

A flicker of a smile twitched the corner of Moriarty's lips, only to be replaced at once by his normal impassivity. "Thank you, miss, but I rather enjoy my present position and its attendant privileges and amusements. It is my pleasure to serve you." He bowed deeply, seated Professor Lepworthy, and then stepped back to stand at his usual attention.

The professor handed the bottle and envelope to Uncle Augustus. "For you, Augustus, as a token of appreciation from our Panamanian friends. Generalissimo Reyes-Cardoza is something of an entomologist himself. Jolly chap. We had a lovely conversation last evening."

Uncle set the dark amber bottle on the table next to *Insectile Creatures*, where they both looked quite out of place among the Spode china, crumpets, and cucumber sandwiches. He opened the envelope and removed a letter. He read for a moment, then flung the letter on the table. His countenance crumbled into what seemed to be grief, then he departed precipitously into the shrubberies.

I blinked, astonished at Uncle's behavior. "Professor Lepworthy, whatever has upset Uncle Augustus so?"

"The old egg looked rather unhappy," said James.

"Indeed he did," said Jane, staring thoughtfully after Uncle.

Professor Lepworthy looked as unhappy as Uncle. "I am so sorry, Miss Arbuthnot. I thought your uncle would be

190

pleased with the generalissimo's gift, or I would not have brought it."

James examined the bottle's label. "I take it that this contains the Tou-eh-mah-mah beetle antidote."

"And the letter tells how to use it. Is that correct?" said Jane.

"Yes," said the professor.

I failed to see what had upset Uncle. I was overjoyed. "Why, that's marvelous! It is the answer to our problem. Uncle need not be ashamed to go out in public, nor will I," I exclaimed, thinking of my cherished plans for a London season and the necessary presence of a guardian who was not one of my aunts, which fact had been threatened by Uncle's transformation and new obsession.

Then I remembered the torment on Uncle's face and his sudden departure into the shrubberies. He, quite obviously, did not consider the gift of the antidote a salubrious one. In light of Uncle Augustus's misery, my excitement evaporated like the dew on a summer's morn. I sighed deeply. "However, if it makes Uncle wretched to effect such a cure . . ." I broke off, unable to finish the thought and very much as miserable as Uncle seemed to be.

I glanced at Jane and James, who were seated on either side of me, for some support. Jane took my hand in hers while James patted me on the shoulder. His touch helped me smile tremulously and say, "I cannot think what must be done. If I am happy, then Uncle is unhappy, and if Uncle is happy, then I . . ." I worried my lower lip between my teeth as I studied the arboretum where the foliage quivered suggestively.

Jane, James, and Professor Lepworthy turned in their chairs to look in the same direction. At that moment Uncle leaped to the head of a piece of statuary and from there to the top of a nearby reproduction of a Greek temple, where he snatched something from the air and then disappeared into the surrounding vegetation.

"Magnificent," said Professor Lepworthy.

"Such agility is quite unusual in a man his age," said Jane, her eyes wide in astonishment. I realized she had not previously seen Uncle in action.

James nodded. "Pity to lose such an ability."

Just then the shrubberies parted, and Uncle Augustus trudged purposefully toward us. He stopped just short of the table and faced us, taking a determined stance—chin high, hands clasped behind his back, eyes fixed just over our heads—looking every bit the distinguished English gentleman whom I had known and loved my entire life. Even so, he seemed somewhat wilted.

He cleared his throat and said, "I have been thinking it over and come to a conclusion. It is not only my duty to care for my dearest niece until she comes of age, it is my wish to do so as well as is possible, because of the great affection I have for her." For a moment his chin quivered. Then he took a deep breath and continued resolutely, "Therefore I will take the antidote and follow the ritual directions to the letter in order to restore normality."

"Oh, Uncle," I exclaimed as I jumped up from my chair and embraced him. His arms came around me, and he drew me into an embrace.

I pulled myself away to gaze up into his face. "No, I cannot allow you to do so."

"What?" he said, clearly confused. "Why ever not?"

"Because, dearest of uncles, I love you too much, and I want you to be happy more than I could ever want a London season."

"But . . . but . . ." He seemed at a loss as to how to counter my declaration.

"Professor Lepworthy," said James. "Do you know if eating a Tou-eh-mah-mah beetle can cause any detrimental effects other than those exhibited by Mr. Percival? Is his condition life threatening?"

"Why, no. In fact the aborigines of Tou-eh-mah-mah Island have unusually long life spans. Several scientists attribute this to their beetle ingestions, which many of them do in a coming-of-age ritual. It has not been proven that the beetles are the actual cause of aboriginal longevity. However, we do not know the effects of beetle ingestion on those who are not Tou-eh-mah-mah natives," said Professor Lepworthy.

"So we do not know for certain if Uncle's condition is ultimately beneficial or detrimental? Now I truly am confused as to what we should do," I said.

"Ahem," said Uncle Augustus. "As I said, for my niece's sake, I am willing to make the sacrifice of—"

"Perhaps I may offer a solution," said Moriarty, gliding to our sides. We watched in astonishment as he pulled a new Vile Vial from his pocket and set it on the table with a flourish.

Both James and Jane started up from the table, putting some distance between themselves and the Vile Vial, although Professor Lepworthy regarded it with mild interest, obviously not having encountered it previously. Uncle and I prudently stepped back a pace.

Moriarty seemed to find our actions amusing. His lips twitched, and I gained a glimmer of understanding about why he enjoyed butlering in my household. He continued, "You see upon the table the small bottle in which I keep my most useful"—and here he could not help but momentarily smile—"smelling salts. You will notice that the cork stopper keeps the contents from spilling, which makes the bottle convenient for carrying on my person at all times.

194

Moriarty bowed and clicked his heels once more. "You can count on me, miss. I would not be absent from such events for the world."

"Although I can't imagine what else could possibly happen," I said.

Perhaps several such bottles would be suitable—properly labeled with directions for carrying out the ritual, of course—for Miss Arbuthnot, myself, and Mr. Percival to have on our respective persons for the possible contingency of an emergency when we would have to administer the antidote. Then Mr. Percival might safely continue in his present state."

"Brilliant," said Uncle as he gave a small leap into the air and came down clutching a dragonfly. He grinned hugely, chewed it, and swallowed.

"Bravo," shouted James as he hugged me to his side. I would have preferred a kiss but contented myself by hugging him in return.

Jane could not help laughing with the rest of us at Uncle's antics.

Much as I enjoyed being in James's arms, I disengaged myself and turned to my butler. "And bravo to you, Moriarty. You are truly brilliant. In fact, you are a butler among butlers."

Moriarty bowed and clicked his heels, in the manner of the generalissimo. "I aim to please, miss."

"You do. Very much so. And I hope you will remain with us no matter what other unforeseen events may occur," I said, remembering with some dismay my reflections on the difficulty of finding good servants.

195

Perhaps several such bottles would be suitable—properly labeled with directions for carrying out the ritual, of course—for Miss Arbuthnot, myself, and Mr. Percival to have on our respective persons for the possible contingency of an emergency when we would have to administer the antidote. Then Mr. Percival might safely continue in his present state."

"Brilliant," said Uncle as he gave a small leap into the air and came down clutching a dragonfly. He grinned hugely, chewed it, and swallowed.

"Bravo," shouted James as he hugged me to his side. I would have preferred a kiss but contented myself by hugging him in return.

Jane could not help laughing with the rest of us at Uncle's antics.

Much as I enjoyed being in James's arms, I disengaged myself and turned to my butler. "And bravo to you, Moriarty. You are truly brilliant. In fact, you are a butler among butlers."

Moriarty bowed and clicked his heels, in the manner of the generalissimo. "I aim to please, miss."

"You do. Very much so. And I hope you will remain with us no matter what other unforeseen events may occur," I said, remembering with some dismay my reflections on the difficulty of finding good servants.

Moriarty bowed and clicked his heels once more. "You can count on me, miss. I would not be absent from such events for the world."

"Although I can't imagine what else could possibly happen," I said.